CW00345340

SEARCH FOR THE HOLY WHALE

SELENA JANE

The Rose
Press

ABOUT THE AUTHOR

Selena Jane is from Loughborough, England. Her childhood memories and love of animals colour her books as does her passion for travelling.

She now lives in South East Queensland, Australia with her husband, two children and as many animals as she can squeeze onto their small acreage.

To find out more about Selena head over to
www.selenajane.com

Newsletter, comments or questions
email: selena@selenajane.com

Title: Search for the Holy Whale

Author: Selena Jane

www.selenajane.com

Copyright © Selena Jane 2020

All rights reserved. This book or any portion thereof may not be reproduced or used in any manner whatsoever without the express written permission of the publisher except for the use of brief quotations in a book review.

This is a work of fiction. Names, characters and places are a product of the author's imagination, any resemblance to actual persons, living or dead or locals is entirely coincidental.

A catalogue record for this book is available from the National Library of Australia

ISBN: 978-0-6488120-0-5 (paperback)

ISBN: 978-0-6488120-1-2 (ebook)

Publisher: Ink Rose Press www.inkrosepress.com

Cover design : Hannah Linder Design

For my daughter Eve my firstborn love

CONTENTS

WAVE WIPE OUT

*S*ari stared at the exposed seafloor; her heart hammered in her chest. Dying fish slapped the sand, gasping for air. She knew what the receding ocean meant; she'd seen this before.

'Is it the end of the world?' Perak whispered.

She took her brother by the shoulders and pushed him towards the shade of the nearest tree.

'It's another great wave, our game is finished now, no more hiding. Stay here.'

Sari ran along the sand, shading her eyes, and scanned the beach for their parents. She saw them farther along the beach, hand in hand, staring at the empty void where the water once foamed.

'Run,' she cried out to them. 'Run, I've found Perak. Run.'

Her words tore away on the wind.

Stranded canoes littered the seafloor. Fishermen ran towards her. It looked to Sari as if the ocean had been sucked back into itself only to stand on its hind legs, bend over and barrel back towards the shore. Her parents turned and ran as the wave thundered back toward them, racing across the ocean floor.

A horn blared.

Turning back to Perak, she screamed as she ran towards him, 'climb quickly, now.'

She shoved her brother so hard he lost his footing, and she grabbed his foot to balance him.

She screamed above the wave's ferocious roar. 'Cross your arms and legs around the tree like me, see? Do it now.'

Her breath came hard and fast now as she watched the enormous wave approach, black and menacing, foaming and frothing.

Perak whimpered as he positioned himself. She pushed her forehead against his and stared into his eyes. 'Close your eyes, and don't let go, promise.'

He closed his eyes. The roar filled her ears and she felt the sting of the spray before the wave hit the tree. She squeezed her eyes shut. The violent shuddering of the tree coursed through her body and she felt its trunk bend so far back it touched the tree behind it. The water, icy cold, slapped the air from her body, forcing her eyes open, and the sting of the saltwater burned her eyes. Perak screamed, and Sari's mouth filled with water as she joined him. She ducked instinctively, pulling Perak's head with hers, as a large branch cracked and tore away, narrowly missing their heads. Her cheek slammed into the rough bark of the tree, and a sob escaped her lips. She clamped her teeth together in pain. The water slapped, pushed and pulled as it forced its will upon them. Sari rocked and bumped against the tree as she pressed her knees into the bark while concentrating on keeping her ankles crossed. Her arms looped around the tree and behind her brother's back, where her fingers dug deeply into her wrists, where they met. The water dragged everything along with it. Out of the corner of her eye, Sari saw bodies being dragged back out to sea. The canoes and fish went with them. Perak continued to scream as the water turned and rushed back towards the ocean, and the force pulled them away from the tree.

'Turn around and face the other way,' she screamed above the roar. 'Hold on now; it's going back.'

He stopped screaming, but he was frozen to the spot, his eyes pleading with her to make it stop.

'I will not let you fall.'

He looked down at the swirling water and back up at her.

'Please, Perak.'

Perak's legs swung free as he held on with only his arms. Sari grabbed his elbows as relief swamped through her body.

Another wave came crashing towards them. They turned to face it and Perak crossed his legs once more. Palm fronds, branches, canoes, bodies, and debris crashed past them. A series of waves washed in and out, slapping them against and away from the tree.

Finally, the waves became calmer, and the muddy water wallowed and swirled around and below them. Their tight grip relaxed around the tree. Perak threw his arms around her neck, and Sari held him as he shook.

'It's all right now, but we must move up again,' she soothed as the water rose to meet them.

He shook his head. 'Nah, I'm so tired, Sari; it's too high.'

'We must, the water's rising. I'm right here, so don't be afraid.'

Her wet-brown locks slapped her face as she tried to pry his arms from her neck.

'I want Mama.'

'Please Perak, Sari wants to keep you safe for Mama, and it's just a little farther now. We might see Mama and Papa from up there,' she said, pointing to the highest branch above them.

* * *

*T*he sun dipped behind the ocean as Perak climbed. Sari nudged him gently from behind. The sun goddess leaving them made her feel alone. *If the water keeps rising, we will have to swim, but to where?* Her eyes searched the foamy water below. Her stomach churned. Neither of them swam well. In the fading light, she wondered what lay beneath the dark and murky surface.

They settled side by side into the fork of the tree.

'I can't see them.' Perak's small voice crept through the tunnels of her heart and squeezed tightly.

She bit her lip and stroked his sand-caked locks. 'We must stay here a while and then we'll look for them. The last wave was a while ago now, but we must be sure it's stopped before we go down.'

He shivered.

'It's getting dark; let's try to get some rest. I'm sure we'll find them in the morning.' She forced a smile to her lips, but she couldn't stop her hands from shaking.

She rested her chin on his head and allowed her silent tears to fall. *I mustn't let him see my weakness, but I'm only fourteen summers old. How can I be old enough to look after my brother if our parents are gone?* She pressed the thought from her mind and clung to her nine-year-old brother as the water flowed beneath them. His brown, naked body shivered next to her wet tunic, and she pulled him closer to her, covering his pale green eyes with her bronzed, freckled hand.

Numb from the cold, she shifted her small frame. Her arms ached with the effort of clinging to the tree's large branch. Her injured eye started to swell and close.

Sari shuddered, trying to push the memory of Perak's screams from her ears and the images of the wave and floating bodies from her eyes. She knew she should be grateful for surviving the first wave, but the water continued to rise as it came back to the shore, and this now was her main concern. She allowed her mind to settle on her parents as she'd last seen them, and her heart squeezed. *Where were they?* She hadn't seen them after they'd turned to run; she'd been pulling Perak from his hiding place and forcing him to climb the nearest tree. She pushed her thoughts away from them and saw the wave again as it had hit Elok Beach, knocking people off their feet in its fury.

'What about Netro?' Perak murmured as he fell asleep in her arms.

She sighed, thinking of her older brother, Netro. 'He was near the edge of the forest with his friends. I'm sure he's fine. Go to sleep now.'

She took deep breaths to calm herself.

Eerily silent now. Dark shadows leaned. No birds twittered, they'd fled the scene of the crime. *How did her people lose touch with nature's signals?* She knew there would be very few animals among the dead. They would have known the wave was coming and would be safe somewhere. Her thoughts turned to the whales. Maybe the whales had avoided Elok Beach this summer, because they, like the birds, knew a giant wave would soon come and claim them.

A black cloud draped over the moon goddess's face, leaving them to the gloom of night. Despite her wet tunic, Sari dozed. She wondered whether the sun goddess would desert them tomorrow. It seemed fitting that she would.

* * *

She woke, not to birds calling, but to the still dark before dawn. Fear rose from the pit of her stomach. Her heart beat faster, thinking of her parents, and she pressed her eyes shut, forcing the image of her parents to the side. Her eye hurt, her throat burned, and her neck ached from its slumped position. She focused on rubbing her neck as she waited patiently for the sun goddess. She clutched the wooden sun and moon carving, which hung from twine around her neck. Her grandpapa had made it for her when she entered this world. As if on cue, the fingers of the sun goddess crept over Elok Beach, warming Sari's black freckles, which splattered finely over her nose and cheeks. Her face prepared to smile, but the expression died on her lips as Perak woke with a start. She grabbed his arm as he started to fall.

He searched her face, and she shook her head and looked down at the water below her. It had begun to seep away during the night. Devastation lay all around. What remained of their village huts bobbed in the murky water below, thatched roofs floated past, along with debris Sari no longer recognised.

She heard voices calling out to one another in the emerging light. Her spirits lifted.

'Hello?' she called. 'Quickly Perak, the water's nearly gone, it's safe for us to go down now.'

They carefully descended into the black muddy water, reaching up to their knees. A group of boys came running towards them with their feet splashing through the water, stirring up a stinky bog-like smell. Like Perak, they were naked, and Sari averted her eyes from their private places. She knew the boys and held up the palm of her hand to each of theirs in greeting.

'Have you seen my family?' she asked.

The eldest boy, Ku, shook his head as he stroked his shadow skink that clung to his shoulder. 'Sixteen bodies we have placed by the caves. They are not of your family.' He pointed in the direction of the caves.

Sari sighed with relief, feeling a little guilty for it.

'We were lucky this time. It was only a small wave, and there will be many survivors this time. The wave will have taken only those on the beach. Where were your family when it came?' Ku asked.

An image of her parents flashed before her eyes. Her eyes slid over Perak.

'Thank you, may the goddess watch over you,' she said, turning from them, dragging Perak by his hand through the mud toward the trees.

'Be careful and watch where you're going. You could cut your feet,' she scolded as he tripped over a piece of wood, muddying himself up to his chest.

'Where are we going?' he whined, covered now in thick black mud.

'We are going to find Netro.'

They stepped over an upturned canoe bogged in the black mud.

A familiar voice called out. 'Sari, Perak, wait.'

Netro's friend Raden strode toward them with his new shadow fox trotting close behind. Wisps from his plaited dark hair stuck to his smooth olive-skinned face. Sari's eyes flicked to his lean brown legs, muddied, but unscathed. Sari sighed as he enveloped them in his muscular arms.

Towering above them, he spoke in his easy manner above her head. 'I am glad to see you are safe.'

For a moment, she felt safe again, free from the thoughts that tortured her.

Raden stepped back, giving them each a smile filled with perfectly straight teeth.

Pleased that he hadn't mentioned her swollen eye, Sari smiled back, closing her lips self-consciously over the gap in her two front teeth.

'I saw Netro, at the edge of the forest,' he said softly,

taking her elbow before he turned to leave. 'I've got to go now; there is much help needed.'

'Wait, did you really see him?'

'Yes, he is well.'

'Wait… my parents?'

'I thought they were with you, sorry, no,' he said, shaking his head.

Her face fell.

'Are you okay, Sari?'

'We'll be fine, go.'

He seemed to hesitate before she watched his lean frame stride off in the direction in which they had come, negotiating the thick mud with ease.

'Come on.' She dragged Perak behind her towards the edge of the forest.

Netro stood chatting with a friend, hands on hips. She checked him over from a distance. He stood smaller than Raden with dark woolly hair and piercing green eyes, similar to her own. As she watched him, her lips quivered, and her eyes started to fill with tears. Netro roared with laughter as his friend staggered off.

Sari gritted her teeth, her tears no longer threatening to spill. She watched him drop something, bend over, pick it up and shove the object inside his tunic. Sari sighed, hoping he wasn't stealing again. She had no energy to question him about it now.

'Netro?' she called.

He turned, his grin confirming that he was unharmed.

'Sari, did you see that wave?' he called out as they squelched toward him. 'Look at your eye; you look like a monster from the deep.'

Sari poked her tongue out in reply and wished immediately that she'd come up with a better response.

Perak exhaled loudly.

Netro picked him up, throwing him over one shoulder. 'What is this, another black monster from the deep, eh?'

He patted Perak's bottom as he spun him around. Perak would not be soothed.

'What's wrong with him, and where is his tunic?'

'The wave took it. Not so hard, you're upsetting him,' she scolded.

Netro continued, regardless.

'We can't find Mama and Papa. Have you seen them?'

Netro dangled Perak by his ankles. 'I thought they were with you.' He shrugged. 'We'd better find Papa. The clean-up has started, and they'll need all the help they can get. The elders have already called a meeting. Where is everyone?'

Sari's mouth dropped open. 'I thought you said you saw the wave?'

'Sure, I did,' he said, lowering Perak to the ground by her feet.

'You were in that forest again weren't you?' she said, shaking her head. 'You know it is forbidden, Netro. If you had really been here and seen the wave, you would have known that the reason no one is about is because they're probably dead or washed away to who knows where.' She clenched her fists. 'Just take a walk down to the beach, and you'll find bodies hanging in the trees or washed up on the shore.'

He sneered. 'You'd better calm down, or your freckles will pop off your face. The wave didn't ride too far into the forest, so the way I see it, the forest saved me.' He threw his head back and sauntered off, slipping as he went.

Sari stared at Netro's back as he staggered away. Netro, nearing sixteen summers, acted as if he was only six summers old, she thought. Inhaling deeply, she tried to calm herself.

Perak pulled on her arm to follow their elder brother.

Where Netro was going, she didn't know, but she let Perak lead her through the squelching black mud.

* * *

*T*hey searched up and down along the shoreline collecting debris, and the silence between them only lengthened the day. Sari yawned. *What could she say?* No words of wisdom or encouragement came to her lips. She felt miserable. The thought of having to take care of her brothers pressed down heavily upon her. *Where were her parents? There was no sign of them.*

A young villager approached. 'It's time to meet under the golden tree, the order of the council.'

They gave up their search and headed for the meeting place. Sari followed, reluctantly, too exhausted to argue in the dimming light.

Perak pointed. 'Maybe they wait for us there?'

'Yes,' Sari mumbled, with a tight smile.

Sari embraced several villagers. No one had seen her parents.

Her mother's sister spoke to her in hushed tones. 'I have been to where they are keeping the injured and dying. They are not there, and no one has seen them.' She hugged Sari tightly to her slim frame. 'I have spoken to many people today. They were last seen on the beach before the great wave came.' Her pale green eyes filled with tears.

Sari nodded, swallowing over the lump in her throat.

They sat and waited patiently for the meeting to begin. Sari looked around. People's shadow animals flittered around nervously, and many villagers wore cloth bandages. She listened to the muffled sobs of her people and a wave of pain took over her. Sorrow clung to her, and to those around her, no one else would be joining them, including her parents. She knuckled a stray tear, and Perak sobbed quietly into her lap.

Three elders stood before them. Malo, in his simple flowing tunic, the one with the kindest face, asked for quiet and spoke first. 'In the last great wave others were found, some many moons later, so we must not give up hope. The coral reef once again protects us, and the goddess has not forsaken us.'

His silver hair blew in the sea breeze.

Sari studied the elders. *Where were they when the wave hit? They didn't look as if they had even as much as a scratch on their wrinkled olive skin.* Sari looked more closely at their fine clothes and thought back to the talk she had heard about the good food they were rumoured to be eating. Malo wore his old robes and bare feet, but she noticed the other two elders had new robes and sandals.

'The rebuilding will begin in a few days when the sun goddess dries the land,' he continued, smiling.

A male villager called from the gathered crowd. 'What about food, now our crops are all destroyed?'

Another called, 'And everything in storage is ruined.'

'Then we shall live as before from the grace of the ocean,' Malo replied.

Another heckler called out again. 'You told us at the last meeting that the ocean catch is polluted and dangerous to eat. Even the whales don't feed and birth here anymore.'

'Oh, yes.' Elder Malo rubbed his temple.

He looked confused Sari felt sorry for him; he was so ancient, but she trusted him. He no longer had his shadow owl, and she wondered whether he still needed it, especially during these times of trouble.

A low murmur rippled through the crowd. It grew until many were standing and shouting at one another. To Sari's astonishment, Netro rose and called for silence by blowing his shell horn.

The crowd turned to hear him. 'I'll go into the forest and find food; there must be a reason why the whales do not come here anymore. Maybe the forest has the answers, and I'm going to find out. Who will come with me?' he shouted proudly above the din.

The crowd chorused, 'The forest is forbidden, it's dangerous.' Horrified looks showed on their tired faces.

Sari's face matched theirs as she tried to pull Netro down to sit beside her.

Ira, the second elder, stood to address the crowd, and both his slit-like eyes and his shadow snakes eyes bore into Netro. 'You are a brave boy Netro, but no one will enter the forest.'

Sari felt Netro wince at the word boy.

The third elder, Fetu, rose to his feet, his ugly face sneering. He hissed at his shadow rat as it ran up his arm. 'It is not necessary. We will send messengers to other villages, and they will send supplies as they have done before. Now let us discuss other matters.' He waved his hand in dismissal.

With Netro dismissed, Fetu had as usual silenced any rebellion.

A shiver ran down Sari's spine as she saw the look of anger pass over Netro's face. She touched his arm.

'No, I know I'm right,' he hissed, getting up and striding away.

Sari noticed that the elders watched him go.

The meeting went on into the night. Perak yawned. The men signalled to women and children that they could leave them, and with no hut to sleep in, Sari went back to the tree that had saved them.

'Come on, Perak, we'll look for Mama and Papa when the sun wakes.'

A warm breeze enveloped Sari as she climbed the tree. She slept fitfully, dreaming of her parents being washed away.

* * *

*M*oons waxed and waned. Nine villagers had been laid to rest, and thirty-two villagers were still missing, including Sari's parents. The remaining villagers collapsed into their straw beds every night, exhausted from spending their days rebuilding their village.

The siblings walked along Elok Beach. Netro had lost his usual good humour today.

'It's been so long. They're not coming back, are they?' sighed Sari.

Netro grumbled, ignoring her question. 'I know I'm not building any more huts. Hurry, Perak,' he snapped. 'Why don't we move further into the forest? This beach is too open. I can't see why they keep rebuilding when another wave will come, and it will all be washed away again.'

Sari was tired of the same old conversation. 'You know why. They're afraid,' she said.

'I know, I know I've heard it all before; the forest is dangerous. All those who have gone inside it without permission and protection from our wise woman were lost never to return,' he said, rolling his eyes. 'They found paradise in there and didn't want to come back here, that's what really happened.'

Sari's chest squeezed. *Why was her brother so insensitive?* She wanted to change his focus. 'You know I've never shown much interest in these things, tell me again why we can't follow the beach and go around the island, go to a beach that is more protected from the waves?'

'No one can swim around Intan Rock, you know that,' he replied.

They looked north to the shiny black rocks in the distance, jutting out into the ocean.

'Stupid villagers have died on those rocks,' Netro said, shaking his head.

'Why do you call them stupid?'

'They could have gone through the forest, like many tribes before them.'

'Yes, but that was a long time ago before the forest was forbidden.'

'And why is the forest forbidden? Fear, superstition, and control. They want to control us, Sari, can't you see that?' He sighed.

'Netro, if you don't stop with this obsession about the forest, they will banish you. You can't go around accusing people with no proof.'

They walked in silence. Sari had dreamed about other places, and now that their parents were gone, the idea of searching for them seemed more tempting to her.

'What about trying the other way?' She looked to the south.

Netro's voice filled with knowing. 'Grandpapa told me that the beaches to the south are plagued by quicksand and that master builders have tried to build over them, but it didn't work. The forest is the only way.'

'So that's true, about the sand if Grandpapa said it.'

Sari remembered that the menfolk in their hut would spend many hours talking of the forbidden forest. Her grandpapa had been a master fisherman, and he knew all about the legends of the ocean, but the forest was a mystery to them all. They had thrived on gossip mixed with imagination.

Sari looked out over the glint of the sea. 'I wish the whales would come back. I miss them.'

Netro cleared his throat. 'Do you remember Grandpapa telling us stories about the Holy Whale?'

'Yes, but I have never seen it, and I am sure it was in his imaginings. Did you know he once claimed he could talk to it?' Sari smiled again at her grandpapa's memory.

He had passed over last summer. She remembered when she was young and how they would sit at his feet, and he would tell them wild and wonderful stories of his adventures at sea. He had been forbidden to speak about it in his dying years. He claimed he couldn't remember, but Sari knew he had been saving face.

'I remember too,' Perak piped up.

'You were too young, Perak,' Sari said, dismissing him.

'I can too. I can remember Sari,' he sulked, kicking the sand.

'Okay, Perak.'

He had turned very childlike since the wave, and his baby voice grated on her nerves. Until now, Sari had let it go because of their parents, who had always babied him. 'What do you remember?' she snapped.

His pale green eyes widened at her tone. He pulled a sulky face and told them what he recalled almost word for word. 'There is a white whale. Grandpapa called him "The Holy Whale" he is magical and all-powerful. Grandpapa said he spoke to him, and he believed that the white whale went to live in the waters on the other side of the island. And because of this, their land is blessed with great wealth and fortune.'

Netro patted his younger brother's head. 'Our side of the island is cursed. If we could get the Holy Whale to come back here, everything would be okay. Maybe the other whales would follow him back.'

'I know you love the whales, but you don't know that the Holy Whale has anything to do with the disappearance of the other whales or the problems we're having,' Sari said, shaking her head.

'I know he must call to them, and they go to him.'

How Netro knew these things, she would never understand. 'You can't believe that a whale is responsible for all this,' she scoffed, spreading her arms wide.

'Why not? You believe that the forest is cursed. Why can't something be magical? If you believe in the bad, then you must believe in the good,' Netro challenged.

She backed down.

Netro looked long and hard at Sari.

'What is it?' Sari asked, reading the expression on his newly stubbled face. It seemed strange to see him with facial hair, she thought distractedly.

'I want to show you something,' he whispered, looking around. 'It's in the hut.'

2

NETRO'S FIND

*T*he council ruled that they would share a small hut until their parents returned, and Sari felt proud of what they had built. Once inside, Netro reached under his straw mat and produced a round object the size of his palm. It shone with dark silver.

'What is that?' Perak asked, his eyes shining.

'It's a pearl silly,' Sari chided, knowing it was no ordinary pearl.

'A pearl? It's too big for a pearl, I found it the day the wave came,' Netro explained. 'Solid as a rock, but there's something inside it. I can't open it,' he said, giving it to Sari.

She took it from him and rolled it in her hands. It felt icy cold, and she saw no visible opening. She suddenly remembered that Netro had hidden something from her on the same day the wave came; *this must be it*, she thought.

'Me look; I look.' Perak jumped up and down, pumping his arms at his sides, his ever-present pack containing his precious drawings bobbing around on his back.

Sari held it above her head. 'I will show you, Perak, if you promise not to talk in that silly baby voice anymore.'

'I promise.' He puffed out his chest.

After having a quick look, she handed it over to Perak and watched her brothers with amusement as they took turns in prodding, bashing, banging and shaking it. Netro eventually threw it across the hut in frustration, where it slammed against the palm woven wall before hitting the dirt next to Perak, who had given up and sat sulking on the floor. Nothing they did to the pearl broke it or even scratched it.

'Let me have another look,' she said. 'We must be missing something.'

Netro retrieved it and threw it to Sari. She turned the pearl in her hands slowly again and stared at it. She willed something to happen. Then she unfocused her eyes and crossed them. She glimpsed something as her vision blurred again. Letters swam in front of her.

'I can see some letters.'

'Let me see.' Netro leaned over her shoulder and looked closely at the pearl-like object in her hands.

'I can't see anything,' he grumbled.

'You have to cross your eyes and blur your vision. Like this.' She demonstrated by crossing her eyes.

'I can't do it.'

She laughed at his attempt. 'Here, watch me again. Cross your eyes and look at your nose, then take your eyes out of focus.' She demonstrated once more.

Sari placed the dark silver pearl in Netro's cupped hands, and he tried again. She felt guilty for being sharp with Perak earlier and made a funny face for him. He giggled at her antics as Netro practised.

'I see something but can't read it.'

Netro rubbed his eyes from the strain of trying, and Sari had another turn.

'Look there, see the markings, there.' She pointed.

Barely visible in the corner of the pearl, something had been written in a small script.

'I see it! It looks like another language. We need a translator book. Where are Grandpapa's books?' Netro jumped up and turned around, scanning the pile of possessions they had managed to salvage.

'I took all the books to the chamber,' Sari mumbled.

She knew she should have shared this information earlier and looked guiltily to the floor.

'What chamber? Why?' the boys demanded in unison.

'They are using one of the old storage caves. A lot of books were lost in the wave. A messenger came and said all books were to go to a central place, so our history wouldn't be lost. Some will be copied. We can go there any time we like and read books, but they are not to be removed. It was an order of the council,' she rambled.

'Do you always do as you're told, Sari?' Netro glared at her. 'Those books were special.'

'It was an order of the council,' she scowled, 'and yes, unlike you, I do as I'm told.'

'Come then! Let's see this chamber.'

Netro's mood had changed again as he put the pearl into his tunic pocket. Sari felt annoyed and confused by Netro's ability to chop and change his moods.

Netro led the way to the caves with Sari and Perak trailing behind.

'Which one is it?'

'The first one,' she answered.

They knocked on the large wooden door at the foot of the cave. An ancient and tired woman who looked familiar to Sari answered. Her crinkled face creased even more as she greeted them with a smile.

'Lena's children, come. I don't see many visitors. Everyone's a little suspicious of coming here and reading,' she whispered. 'They think I will tell the council what they're reading about.'

Sari became alarmed. 'Would you?'

'That depends,' she cackled. 'You look harmless.'

She led them through a cold passageway where torches lined the walls. Sari pulled her tunic closer to her as they stepped into a large, well-lit chamber. Long tables followed the walls, piled high with books that spilled over onto the floor. Sari knew the way the books were being treated would annoy Netro.

'Don't worry about the mess. I'm still sorting it out. What do you think?' the old woman asked.

No one answered her, but the number of books that had been collected impressed Sari. Over to their right, a vast open fire roared up through an opening in the cave. A boy placed open books in front of the fire, turning the pages to dry them.

'That's my grandson, he'll take the books from your pack.' The old woman looked at Perak and nodded in the boy's direction. 'He can help you with whatever you need. I'm going out back.'

Sari wondered where out back led.

'Oh no, I don't have any books for you, I carry my draw-ings with me to keep them safe,' said Perak

'We'll just look around,' Netro replied, rolling his eyes.

'It will be a long look if you want something special.' The old woman narrowed her eyes.

Sari sensed trouble and smiled as the old woman smiled, patting Perak on the head, 'We were hoping to read Perak here, a bedtime story. He's having trouble sleeping.'

The old lady snorted and shuffled away.

'Don't cause trouble. She knows our mama,' Sari hissed.

Netro glared at her. 'They're our books. I don't need her

permission.' He lowered his voice. 'I haven't seen the boy before. Have you?'

'No, he must be home-schooled. Let's get on with it.'

The boy eyed them warily from across the room while they pretended to browse through a few books.

'You read to Perak, and I'll look back here,' Netro whispered.

She chose several books and read aloud to Perak, who sat beside her on the stone step. She watched Netro wade through piles of books across the chamber. She wasn't the only one who watched him. The boy kept a close eye on him. Sari wondered if he had been told to watch them.

Sari stifled a yawn. She had now read four books to Perak, and Netro had still not found a translator book. She knew they needed the boy's help.

'Do you have any translator books?' she asked casually, feeling Netro's glare boring into her from across the room.

'Why d'you need one?' The boy looked at her suspiciously.

Sari exhaled and shot Netro a look, which she hoped would keep him quiet.

'We lost our parents in the tidal wave, and we were talking today about the meaning of our names. You see my name Sari means "essence".' She pointed to Netro. 'His name means "vision," and well, Perak wants to know the meaning of his name. My parents are not here to help us, so we need the book,' she said, looking down into her hands. 'We could look up your name too if you like.' She looked up and gave him her sweetest smile.

The boy picked up a sizeable bound book at his feet.

'It's damp, so be careful when you turn the pages.'

Netro rolled his eyes as Sari took the book from the boy.

'What's your name? I'll look your name up first as you've been so very kind.' She smiled.

The boy blushed. 'Ulani,' he muttered.

'What a lovely name.' She took the translator book over to the stone steps and sat down with her back to him and flicked through the pages quickly, but carefully. After a few minutes, she had found what she needed. 'Ulani means "happy nature."'

The boy seemed pleased. Studying his face, Sari felt confident that there was nothing happy about his nature. She continued flipping pages. After a few minutes, he wanted the book back and pressed her to hurry.

'Nearly finished,' she assured him and looked wildly at Netro to stall the boy. Netro tried to speak to Ulani about fishing and climbing trees, but he became sullen and insisted she hurry. Sari heard the old women shuffling along the corridor. Ulani strode towards her and snatched the book from her hands, glaring at her.

'How interesting,' she said, getting up. 'Perak means, "silver." Thank you for your help.'

Ulani quickly took his spot by the fire as his grandmamma turned the corner. Netro looked as if he would attack the boy. Sari froze him with a look. Perak fell into his role of being sleepy.

'Looks as though it worked!' The old woman nodded in his direction.

'Yes, thank you,' Sari murmured as they hurried out of the cave.

Night had fallen.

Netro cursed and kicked the cave wall. 'What now?'

'I have what we need.' Sari smirked.

'What did it say?'

'Not here,' Sari said, beginning to enjoy herself.

They raced back to their hut with Sari leading and the boys running to either side of her. It felt good to lead.

'You are so clever, Sari,' Perak gushed.

They burst through the door of their hut. Netro turned to

her once more in their single, round room streaked with moonlight.

'You did well.' Netro smiled at his younger sister and gave her the pearl from his pocket.

She sat down before the unlit fire relishing in her new status.

'Come on, Sari,' they pleaded together.

A wicked smile crossed her lips. 'Perak, close the door, please.'

He got up and did her bidding.

'Light the fire, please, Netro,' she said.

'Aargh, stop it! Come on... if you have it,' he chided, fed up now.

'I need the fire,' she insisted.

He reluctantly got up to light the fire and moaned about girls and their silly games. She waited as he struck the flint together. The fire flickered, and he blew on it gently to get it going. Perak lit the torches from the flame and placed them around the hut. They sat back down and urged her to hurry.

'Come now.'

She turned the pearl over in her hands. 'The inscription reads,' she said dramatically, "If a storm has carried me, a fire will help thee open me."'

They all turned and looked into the burning fire.

Approaching the small fire, Sari held the pearl over its flames. 'Look at this; my hands are hot, but the pearl is still cool.' She pulled her hands away from the heat and held the pearl out for Perak and Netro to touch.

'We need something to hold it over the fire,' Netro said racing outside.

Sari could hear him snapping branches. He came back inside carrying a two-pronged twig. Netro took the pearl from Sari, and, balancing the pearl between its forks, he held it with unsteady hands over the fire. The branch burned through. Netro scrambled to retrieve the pearl as it dropped into the flames.

'It's okay, I've got it,' he reassured, juggling it from hand to hand as it cooled.

A loud knock rapped on their hut door. Sari's mouth dropped, and three pairs of eyes bulged.

'I know you're in there. I can hear you,' a male voice called impatiently.

'It's Raden. Hide it quickly,' Sari whispered. 'I must let him in, or he'll wonder why the door is closed.'

Netro put the pearl into his tunic pocket, where it bulged slightly.

Sari opened the door and knew by the look on Raden's face that he had been listening outside.

'What are you up to?' He grinned, prodding Netro in his taut chest, 'You look as if you got caught with one of the elder's daughters.'

Raden felt like home to Sari; he had helped them rebuild their hut, and they had helped him. Raden lived alone, having reached sixteen summers. He should take a wife, but Raden, like his family for generations before him, resisted the system and lived his own life. Sari was secretly happy that he didn't take a wife. She didn't want to share him outside her own family. His parents had died in the last tidal wave, and maybe this was the reason for her possessiveness. She knew the elders had expelled some of his relatives from the village for speaking out against the elders. Sari suddenly wondered where they had gone. *Funny*, she thought, that this had not occurred to her before. She knew her mind had begun to flower as her grandpapa had told her it would one day, meaning that she would start to think outside herself.

Raden understood their pain of losing their parents and had been of great comfort to them all.

Her attention moved back to the boys as they prodded and poked each other.

Raden noticed the lump in Netro's tunic pocket. 'What have you got in there?' Raden tackled him from behind and held his arms behind his back. Netro being smaller in stature didn't have the strength to hold Raden off for long. Raden applied more pressure until Netro gave in.

'Okay, you can have it. It's no good to you anyway.' Netro handed the pearl over to Raden, who held it in his hand, triumphant for a moment.

Sari saw the look on Raden's face drop. 'What's wrong?'

Raden said, 'we must hide it quickly.' He went to the hut door and slammed it shut and began searching for a place to put the pearl. 'My grandparents had one of these pearls and were expelled from the village. No good can come of it. Where did you get it? Who knows you have it?' he demanded.

'It's good, Raden, no one knows we have it!' Netro assured him.

Raden continued to search.'No. They will find it there,' he muttered to himself.

A scratching sound came from outside, behind the hut door, and they stood still, staring wide-eyed at one another. Raden spun and threw the pearl into the fire.

'Get the door, Perak,' Raden commanded as he stood in front of the fire with his back to it with Sari and Netro standing beside him.

Perak opened the door. Looking down, he groaned. 'It's just your shadow fox.'

A four-legged red-furred animal slunk into the room and went to Raden's side.

Raden shrugged his shoulders. 'Sorry, I'm not used to having a shadow yet.'

* * *

*T*wo full moons had passed since Raden's coming of age ceremony. Sari wondered whether Raden did not like the goddess's choice of a fox for him. *Perhaps he, like Netro, prayed for an eagle.* Before she furthered that thought, the fire behind them burst into light. They jumped clear, four sets of eyes following a rainbow of colours, which burst from the flames and beamed over the hut walls. Strobes of radiant reds and purples rocketed in straight lines, zooming past their heads.

Sari ducked down instinctively.

Jagged beams of brilliant blues and greens zipped past the purples and reds. Streaks of glowing yellow and gold whooshed to join them. Sari gasped at the silent light display before them. The rays of colour swung from left to right, crossing each other, fighting for space on the small ceiling. The swinging beams slowed to a sway and connected.

Raden's shadow fox cowered in the corner of the hut. Sari felt hypnotised by the dancing lights and swayed on her feet. The colours stopped suddenly, and lines began to appear, and shapes formed.

'What is it?' Sari asked.

'Looks like a map,' Netro replied.

'Look!' Perak called. 'The pearl is melting.'

Netro and Raden, trance-like, ignored him.

Sari glanced over in his direction.

Perak went to his special box and got out a tattered square of rag and a piece of black chalk. He sat on the floor and drew, copying the map. He kept an eye on the pearl in the fire as he sketched. He loved to draw, thought Sari as she watched him. He sketched quickly and precisely. The pearl had melted to the size of Sari's finger, but Perak calmly rechecked his work against the dancing lights. The lights above their heads faded.

'It's going; quick, do something,' Netro panicked.

Sari joined Perak. 'Oh, you are so clever.' She checked the lines and formations of his chalked map. 'It's the same,' she said as she hugged him.

The lights above them faded to nothing, and they stared at the moonlit ceiling.

'It's gone,' Netro moaned, sinking to his knees.

Sari looked over at the fire, where the pearl had completely melted away. She nudged Perak and nodded toward Netro. He understood and went over to him, showing him his map.

Netro's eyes lit up. He jumped up, threw Perak over his right shoulder, and spun him around. 'You clever little man, I knew this drawing skill of yours would be important one day.'

Raden hugged Sari, and Netro embraced them both, so they formed a circle with Perak above their heads.

'The map,' Netro reminded them, laughing.

Perak laid the map on the sandy floor, and, sitting in a circle, they studied it.

'How do we make sense of it? We don't even know what the map is of or where it leads to,' Sari pointed out.

'What do you think, Raden?'

'I don't know, but I just know if I follow this map, I will find my grandparents and maybe...' He drifted off.

'How do you know that?' she asked, sadly thinking of her own parents.

'A pearl, just like this one, had something to do with them disappearing. I was meant to find this pearl and to find them. I can't keep waiting for them to return and live in fear that the elders might banish me for not marrying or following their rules.'

Sari heard his words catch in his throat.

'But you didn't find it. I did.' Netro squared his shoulders. 'Maybe it was meant for me?'

Sari shook her head. *Netro could be so stupid*, she thought.

'Okay, well, maybe it was meant for all of us. All I know is a strong feeling that I must follow this map.' Raden studied the map intently.

'Me too,' Netro puffed.

Perak jumped up. 'I'm going too.'

'Wait a minute! No one is going anywhere. The map doesn't even make any sense yet,' Sari reminded them. A fluttering began in her stomach at the thought of leaving the village.

'Where did you find the pearl?' Raden wanted to know.

'At Elok Creek. Let's go there, and I'll show you,' Netro offered, getting up.

'No, it's too dark now. Let's get a good night's rest. I'll come just before sunrise. We can all go together. Remember, not a word to anyone.' Raden left with his shadow fox at his heels.

* * *

*S*ari waited with her brothers at the edge of the forest. She jumped at every pre-dawn sound. They waited impatiently for Raden as the sun goddess addressed the day. Sari yawned. Her brothers' faces looked eager, she knew that like herself they could not sleep, and yet she felt their excitement through their tiredness. She heard footfalls behind her and jumped to find Raden with his shadow fox at his feet.

'I expected you from the east,' she said, trying to cover her jitters.

'I couldn't sleep. I've been looking around. Come Netro, show me where you found it.'

'I dropped it here, but no one saw me pick it up.' Netro pointed to the mist-covered ground at their feet.

'How do you know, no one saw you?' Raden questioned.

'I'm not stupid.' He scowled.

Sari looked away, knowing she had seen Netro pick something up on that day. Netro could be so rude to Raden that sometimes she wondered why they were friends. She kept quiet about what she had seen. The usually calm and relaxed Raden was making her nervous. She didn't want to give him any more reason to get anxious.

They followed Netro into the forest. She hoped they wouldn't go anywhere near the boundary where it is forbidden to cross. She wondered how many times Raden and Netro had crossed the boundary and how far they had ventured beyond its border. Sari felt the temperature drop as they continued along the narrow muddy path in single file. She wasn't happy about being last in the line and tried to concentrate on the three dark heads bobbing in front of her as she walked. The trees were thick with foliage, but Sari could still see the pale-yellow sky through the tall trees. It was quiet, but she felt forest eyes upon her as she stumbled along.

The sound of running water up ahead signalled their arrival at Elok Creek. The swell of the creek was much larger than she remembered. Large moss-covered boulders crowded together, creating a waterfall, and water splashed into the creek from both sides where a smaller pile of rocks crammed together, collecting dead leaves. Netro showed them where he had found the pearl.

'Just here next to these smaller rocks.' He pointed.

Raden studied the map as he walked.

Sari smiled to herself as she watched Netro and Perak follow him. Netro scratched his head.

'Can I help?' she offered.

'Girls are not good at map reading,' Netro teased.

She'd like to show them, she thought and sat down on a patch of damp grass and unpacked her sack. Listening to her stomach growl, Sari arranged some star fruit on a plate woven from coconut fibre. The boys joined her. Netro filled his pitcher from the creek and shared the cold water around.

'Any luck?' she asked.

'We can't see anything that looks like what's on this map. We must be in the wrong place,' Netro said, throwing the map to her. 'Go on. I know you're dying to show us.'

Sari ignored him and studied the map. She looked up at the creek and back at the map.

Raden pointed to a shaded section on the far right of the map. 'Suppose this is Intan Rock. That would be northeast. Follow it south along what would be the beach and our village.' He showed her with his finger. 'Go inland to the west into what should be the forest, but there's no creek shown on the map. We are looking for this symbol with the three prongs. It should be here where we're standing, but it's not.'

Sari studied the symbol. It looked like a snake with three heads; she decided. She looked up at the creek again.

'We can't see anything that looks like this three-fingered thing,' Netro mumbled, biting into a turtle egg.

She glared at him. 'Raden has just explained that. Why do you always speak to me as if I'm stupid?'

Netro stuck out his tongue, covered in chewed egg.

They sat silently for a while as Sari tried to ignore Netro's face-pulling antics.

'What if the creek wasn't here when the map was made? Maybe the map's old,' she suggested.

'How does that help us?' Netro rolled his eyes.

'Maybe that three-pronged thing is under the water,' she mumbled, unsure of herself.

Netro eyes widened. Then he jumped up, pulling his tunic over his head as he ran to the water. Sari ran to the water's edge with Raden and Perak and watched as Netro dived down into its green depths with a splash. He came up quickly, gasping for air.

'It's cold and much deeper than it looks.' He took a deep breath and dived down again.

Sari stared at the water, trying to see into its depths.

Netro came up for air.

'What do you see?' she shouted.

Ignoring her, he took several deep breaths and continued to dive. He swam into the middle of the creek, then to the far right and then over to the far left, diving at each point.

'I guess I was wrong; stupid idea really.' Sari felt annoyed at herself.

'Ah! Sari, you always doubt yourself. Wait and see,' Raden chided.

Netro swam to the creek's rim and waded out of the water, wearing a grin wider than Raden's shadow fox, which lay on its back, wriggling about in the leaves.

'You were right, Sari! It looks like a huge tree split into three under the water. It's all black on the ends; maybe struck by lightning.' He shook his wild locks and groped for his tunic.

They ran back to the patch of grass to study the map again. Raden took charge once more. The map showed an arrow pointing west from the middle prong.

'Which way was the middle prong facing?' Raden asked.

Netro pointed into the forest. 'Right where the map shows us.'

They were excited now.

'So, when do we go?' Perak wanted to know.

Sari held up her hand, 'You are too young to come and don't complain that Mama wouldn't like it. If we decide to go, you will stay in the village and wait for us to come back.'

Perak pulled a face, and she childishly pulled a face in return.

'I'm not too young! Tell her, Netro.'

Netro looked away as he dressed.

'What does he mean, Netro?' Sari had that same feeling she always had with Netro when he was keeping something from her.

'He's nine summers old, it'll be okay,' Netro ventured, not looking at her.

'No, he's too young! Besides, we haven't decided on anything yet.' She flipped her waist-long hair in defiance.

'Well, I'm going,' Raden said.

'I'm going too!' Perak jumped to his feet. 'You wouldn't even have a map if it weren't for me. Anyway, I've been past the boundary before, and I can do it again.'

Sari leapt to her feet, opened her mouth to shout at Perak, and closed it again, turning on Netro. 'You!' she spat. 'You took him in there, and it's forbidden!'

Sari screamed with such passion she made herself jump. 'This betrayal is too much, how could you keep this secret from me?' Sari marched off toward the creek where she knelt and splashed water on her face and let the hot tears flow. She felt someone behind her, and Raden placed his hand lightly on her shoulder.

'Sari, he's not a baby anymore. You don't have to be his mother because his mother is gone.'

She ignored him, biting her lip.

'Be his sister and help him become a man.'

She turned to him, wiping her face with her sleeve. 'I'm responsible for them if anything happens...' she mumbled.

'No one is responsible. We are a family. We look out for

each other, but we each have our own destiny. No one can change that. Netro has adventure running through his veins, he is passionate about the forest and its secrets. It's okay that he wants to influence Perak.'

She realised he was right. Perak had come to no harm. She took a deep breath and felt calmer; the anger slipping away.

'I'm scared,' she confessed, looking into his warm brown eyes.

'Fear is not real. Life has great plans for you, Sari. You'll see.'

He squeezed her shoulder gently.

She felt a little embarrassed now by Raden's wisdom and her lack of it. She looked over to her brothers and smiled weakly. She joined them with Raden. Perak put his head on her shoulder as she put her arm around him. Netro rolled his eyes, and she ignored him.

'Okay, so when do we go?' she asked, smiling.

She knew deep in her heart that she could not have left Perak behind.

'Let's go now,' Perak squealed.

'We need supplies, silly monkey.' She rubbed his curls.

Raden took charge of the organising. They spent a long time discussing what each of them would bring.

'What do we tell our families?' Sari wanted to know.

'I say we go telling no one,' Raden said.

Raden had very little family, so he would say that, thought Sari.

'Just disappear. I like it,' Netro agreed.

'We can't do that. We should tell someone!' Sari gave them a disapproving look.

'What if they followed us and captured us? Then we will never find out what happened to our families or to the whales, and we will be in trouble with the elders,' Sari said, shaking her head. 'If we disappear, they will look for us, but if we leave a message with someone to tell them we have gone beyond the border, they will not follow. We could leave in the middle of the night, and that way by dawn when they are told we will be far into the forest.' Bumps crawled up her arms at the thought. 'I'm not going to just disappear.'

Raden studied Sari's face, and she blushed under his stare. 'Okay, Sari, we'll do it your way. Who do you trust? Who won't try to stop us or turn us in to the elders?'

'What about Heni?' Sari asked.

Raden nodded. 'Heni is a good choice. You and Perak can be in charge of telling Heni and organising the food for the first part of the journey. Just remember, we will have to carry what you pack.' He pointed at Netro. 'We will gather what we need for hunting, protection, and anything else we can think of. Does everyone agree that we will leave tonight?'

'Yes,' they chorused.

'Let's get back to the village, and no talking to anyone but Heni about this, especially you, Perak.'

That remark caused a fresh round of sulks from Perak, but Sari had no time to deal with Perak now. Her mind spun. She had food to prepare, and she had too many things to do and to think about. She mulled words over in her mind as they walked back through the forest. *How would she approach Heni, what would she say to her? How would Heni react?* Perak stumbled in front of her. *Would he be safe?* They all had different reasons for wanting to make this journey. For Perak, she guessed it was about the adventure. He wanted to grow up and be like his brother and Raden. Sari exhaled. She had told the boys she wanted to find out what had happened to the whales, and while this was partly true, she secretly hoped to find her parents. Sari longed to see them again. She prayed for a miracle. She believed that if she prayed hard enough and long enough, they would come back to her.

Rubbing her sun and moon necklace between her fingers, she thought of Raden; he hoped to find his grandparents. *Could he still harbour that wish after all these years?* She hoped not, but then scolded herself inwardly. He had as much right as she did to believe his grandparents were still alive. Raden gave her a wink, and her cheeks burned with guilt. Sari had to remind herself that he couldn't read her mind.

Netro fell into line in front of her as the path narrowed. She wondered about his reasons for wanting to go. He probably saw himself as a hero, she thought, and she groaned inwardly.

3

WINGED WAR

*T*he day passed quickly into the night. Sari double-checked the items she had prepared for the journey. If she had forgotten something, they would just have to manage, but she didn't want to show any weakness in front of the boys. She thought of brave Heni, who had cried but had promised to do anything to help Sari.

Netro grumbled about the moon goddess showing her full face. 'She's too bright. How will we leave without being seen?'

They sat in their hut, waiting for cloud cover.

Raden emptied their sacks to pass the time. 'You won't need these drawings, Perak.'

Sari wasn't happy about him going through her belongings, and Perak looked miserable.

'Sari, you don't need a pouch of sand.' He chuckled.

'It will remind me of home,' she said, blushing again.

Netro rolled his eyes.

'Every little thing will add weight to your pack. The forest will provide for us. You'll see,' Raden added patiently.

She let him get on with it. Picking up her pack later, she

had to admit it felt lighter and more manageable. She was glad that Raden had taken on the leadership role. While eating a large meal of fresh fish and sweet potato with figs and honey for dessert, Sari felt sleepy. The idea of venturing into the cold dark forest had become less appealing to her as she sat by the warmth of the fire, absently plaiting her long brown hair.

Raden whistled for his shadow fox. 'Okay, we have good cloud cover now; let's go.'

Walking into the balmy night air, whereby every sound seemed to shrill through Sari's small frame, she looked back at their small hut some distance away. 'Goodbye,' she whispered.

They heard voices at the edge of the forest and slipped quietly into the coverage of the trees. Following the same path that they had travelled earlier that morning, Sari felt comforted by its familiarity. She insisted that she and Perak travel in the middle of the line, that Raden take the lead, and Netro bring up the rear.

The cloud cover vanished, and the full face of the moon goddess lit their way. They reached Elok Creek's lagoon and chose their path facing west. The track was clear of over-hanging branches, but it squished with mud underfoot, and Perak slipped on rotting leaves in front of her. She caught him by the arm. It smelt mouldy and damp. Sari missed the smell of the ocean, but the excitement had overtaken her fear, and she no longer jumped at every night noise. Elok Creek slipped farther behind them, and Sari no longer felt sleepy.

Raden stopped up ahead with his shadow fox at his heels. They had reached the border.

When Sari joined him, she looked down at the pickets at her feet. 'Is this it?'

Sari had never seen the border before, having gone only

as far as the creek to collect fresh water when supplies were low closer to their village. Sari felt cheated. She'd expected a huge wall or barrier that they would have to scale. It wasn't even a small fence, just a line of pickets spaced a few feet apart, which she stepped over easily.

'I guess the elders believed no one would dare to cross.' She sighed, disappointed somehow.

Sari wasn't sure if she felt upset with herself for crossing or for never crossing before. She recognised the anger she felt toward the elders, especially Ira and Fetu, who were always so stern, and hardly noticed the thickening of the trees as they forged ahead.

Raden kept up a steady pace, putting the village farther and farther behind them. They still followed a narrow path, and Sari wondered how there could be a path if no one had ventured this far past the border before.

Raden answered her silent thought. 'This path will lead to a clearing where we will rest for the night.'

Sari had her answer. The boys had been this way before. 'And after that?' she wanted to know.

'We've never been further than the clearing, not west, anyway.'

'So, there will be no path?'

'I don't know.' He shrugged.

Perak dragged his feet. Sari caught some yellow eyes staring at her through the trees and felt relieved to arrive at the clearing.

'No fires this close to the border,' Raden instructed.

Sari unrolled her straw mat with a flourish and placed it carefully over the damp leaves. She noticed Netro rolling his eyes.

'You'll be sorry now that you don't have a mat,' she said. 'The leaves are damp.'

Her straw mat had been something she had not been willing to give up. It had rolled up neatly and had attached nicely under her sack. It wasn't heavy, and she didn't see why she couldn't bring it. Despite the mat, Sari sighed; sleep would not comfort her tonight. She rolled on her back and looked at the full face of the moon goddess. *Why had the moon goddess let her grandpapa die and now her parents?* Sari turned her face away from the moon and focused on a fine spray of stars that lit the inky sky. Sari's eyes felt heavy. Raden's shadow fox tried to get on her mat, and she shooed him away. She heard Perak snoring quietly beside her, and she drifted off to join him.

* * *

Sari woke to the sound of the boys' voices whispering among themselves. They studied the map carefully. The brightness of the day surprised her. She couldn't remember the last time she had missed seeing the sun goddess rise. She lay listening to the birds twittering in the trees and the loud buzzing of insects while keeping one ear on the boys' conversation.

'We need to go straight through there,' said Raden.

They stood with their backs to Sari, staring at a massive wall of tall trees thick with foliage.

'It will be rough going, so lucky I brought this.' Grinning, Netro pulled out a large machete, a blade of black rock filed long and sharp with its handle carved from wood and wrapped tightly with cloth and twine for grip.

Raden had made a similar blade and showed his knife to Perak.

Netro dug into his sack and pulled out two small hunting knives. 'I made these for you and Sari. You can have yours now, and I'll give one to Sari when she wakes up,' he said, giving one to Perak.

He placed the small knife, made from similar materials to his own, into Perak's hand.

Perak jabbed the air between them and then hugged Netro, 'thank you.'

Netro turned back to Raden. 'We should have left Sari at home. She'll never keep up with us and anyway she doesn't like change. Who knows what waits for us in there?' He nodded his head towards the wall of trees.

'She needs this. She's nearly a woman. Don't worry about her. She's strong like your mama,' Raden said, patting Netro on the shoulder.

Sari yawned loudly. 'I'm awake.'

She didn't like them discussing her. She tied her hair back as she walked toward them. Netro handed her the knife.

'Thank you, but what will I need it for? You boys are in charge of the hunting.'

'You might need to protect yourself.'

'I can look after myself,' she replied tartly, popping the knife into her tunic pocket.

They turned their attention back to the wall of trees.

'Are we really going in there?' Sari realised the real journey was about to begin.

Raden turned to her. 'We should eat breakfast and get going. It will be a really hot day.'

She realised they had been waiting for her and quickly went about preparing a simple breakfast of bread and jam from their supplies. Perak whittled on some sticks, and she had to hurry him along.

'There, I'm finished.' He held four sticks, each sharpened on one end. 'For your teeth,' he explained.

'Good idea, thank you,' she said.

They each took one, and Sari realised that Perak was proud of himself for contributing.

Netro and Raden took the lead. They hacked at the dense forest, trying to make a pathway. Sari cleaned her teeth lazily as she walked. The boys ahead sweated and panted with the effort. A bird shrieked overhead, and Sari jumped, dropping her tooth stick.

'I'll make you another one,' Perak offered.

Sari and Perak took over with the machetes for a short time, but their arms tired quickly. Sari felt grateful for the cool of the forest, but the bugs were biting her ankles, and she bent down often to scratch her legs. They stopped for a break. Unable to sit, they stood and drank from their flasks. Sari had become accustomed to the constant buzzing. Netro had explained that it was the noise of thousands of insects rubbing their legs together, a fact she presumed he got from one of his teachers. She watched a large centipede marching to its own beat. She tried to count its legs, but they were too busy. Netro surprised Sari; he seemed different to her in here, almost as if he belonged. He appeared in control and took his role very seriously though she had always thought of him as irresponsible.

They moved on. Sari stumbled in a small animal hole and Perak caught her arm. Her thoughts turned to the village. She wondered if Heni had told anyone yet. She worried about her best friend; *would the elders punish her?* Sari knew her mother's sister would fear for her and Perak. The men in the family would be concerned, but Sari suspected that they would be proud. The village had suffered terribly in the wave. The villagers were struggling to provide food for their families. She knew that unless they could somehow help, her tribe would not make it through the next season without supplies.

She looked down at her legs, covered in scratches and bites. Her legs were starting to shape more like her mama's, she thought, and her heart squeezed. She felt sure she was alive. She collided with Perak's back as he and the other boys halted. Sari looked over his shoulder to see a huge snake hanging from a tree just inches from Netro's face. Sari put her hand to her mouth to suppress the scream. They kept still. Sari had never seen a land snake before, though she had come across sea snakes, they had studied forest animals in school, and she stared at its broad head and slender body, the colour of wet mud. It coiled its length along a large branch, and Sari wondered absently whether even a tidal wave could have washed it away. She doubted it by the way it clung so tightly. She hardly dared to breathe.

Bright yellow scales made bands of yellow through its brown surface. Black eyes fixed on Netro from the sides of its yellow spotted head, and yellow bars striped its upper lip, where its forked tongue flickered in and out. Moments passed. Sari prayed it would move on, but it stayed staring and flickering its tongue. She heard Raden whisper something to Netro. In two quick movements, Netro fell to the floor. The snake bared its hollow fangs at the front of its jaw and Raden swiped at the snake with his long knife and hacked off its head. Netro quickly moved aside as the snake uncoiled and fell to the floor, still quivering with life. Raden's shadow fox leapt at the snake and began devouring it with his needle-sharp teeth. Sari felt disgusted and turned her head away. She prayed that when she came of age that the gods would choose a gentler animal to be her guide and companion.

'That was close,' Netro said through a strangled laugh.

Sari plastered a fake smile on her face. 'Did you see how his nostrils were on the side of his head, not on the top like our sea snakes?'

Sari hoped she showed the confidence she did not feel. She squeezed Perak's hand. He looked as ill as Sari felt. She thought he might be sick, or maybe she would be.

When the fox was done, Raden patted him on the head. 'Good boy. Are you okay, Sari?' Raden asked.

He smiled reassuringly as if he were used to seeing snakes all the time.

'Yes, okay,' she lied.

Nothing seemed to bother Raden.

He took the lead with his shadow fox trotting proudly beside him. Sari took a spot behind Raden and moved at a faster pace, trying to distance herself from the memory of those piercing black eyes.

* * *

The morning dragged, and Sari's stomach rumbled, but before she could voice a complaint, Raden fell through the trees in front of her and rolled down a grass-covered bank. He landed on his back in a circular field of green grass, encircled by tall trees.

'Oh, goddess above, are you all right?' Sari called.

Raden waved a hand in reply but stayed on his back until Netro ran down the grassy hill and jumped on top of him before helping him to his feet. Sari followed with Perak. She had never seen anything more beautiful; the wind caressed the grass, and the fresh air caressed her face. The grass smelled sweet, and Sari drew the scent into her nostrils, where it lingered and settled. She took off her sandals and scrunched her toes between the soft green blades.

'Isn't it wonderful? Let's rest and eat here,' she gushed and felt herself redden under Netro's mocking stare.

They joined her to eat turtle eggs and maize. Raden cracked open two coconuts, sharing the liquid around before cutting out the flesh. Sari shoved a turtle egg in her mouth and took to her feet and skipped in the lush green grass. She twirled around and did a little dance for their entertainment. Raden clapped, and Perak giggled. Sari stopped abruptly and hopped on one foot.

'Ouch, ouch.' She looked under her raised foot as she hopped.

'That'll teach you!' Netro mocked.

She bent down to pull a piece of whitish-grey broken bone from her sole. She rubbed the spot where it had pierced her flesh. She tried to show the bone to her brothers, but they continued to laugh at her as she hopped.

'Let me see,' said Raden.

She showed him her foot.

'Not your foot, the bone.'

'Oh,' she said a little disappointed that no one seemed to care about her foot.

Raden studied the bone carefully. 'It's only a splinter, and it's too hard to tell who or what it came from.'

Chewing on a piece of coconut, he turned the bone over in his hand and cast it aside.

'You should put your sandals on. Could be snakes in that grass,' Raden said, concern in his voice.

Netro rolled his eyes, and Sari poked her tongue out at her brother. She put her sandals back on.

'You are such a girl.' Netro jabbed her in the side.

'I'd rather be a girl than you.' As usual, her comeback was weak, and she knew it.

Raden spoke softly to her as if trying to gauge her mood. 'Let's keep moving. We will need to fetch more supplies.'

Sari gave him her best smile and took Perak's hand. Looking up at the clear blue sky, the four companions walked along next to each other across the clearing.

They came across a small pile of bones and stopped. Raden studied the bones once more.

'Looks like a small animal, maybe a rat,' he said.

Netro crushed a small skull underfoot as they walked. They were stopping every few paces picking over bones, mostly small ones, but some were quite large.

A shiver crept across Sari's skin. 'Oh, this lovely place is like a burial ground.'

Raden picked up another bone, larger than the others. He studied it with interest.

'This is human.'

Perak's eyes widened. Sari registered his look as her mind let it sink in.

'Let's get out of here; there's something about this place.' She took Perak's hand and urged him forward.

An ear-splitting screech echoed through the clearing. Sari ducked down instinctively, taking Perak with her. Raden's shadow fox barked defiantly.

'It's only an eagle. Probably spotted a mouse or something,' Raden assured her.

She rose, spotting the eagle to the north.

'What's that, its family?' Netro pointed to a vast dark cloud moving toward them at high speed.

They watched for a moment as the silent cloud dipped and swayed. Raden's shadow fox flattened his body to the ground with his ears flat against his head and whimpered.

'I don't like this.' Raden said, almost to himself before commanding that his shadow fox rise up and show courage.

Sari grabbed Perak and propelled him forward toward the trees on the other side. 'I'm not waiting around to see what it is.'

'Nah, I want to see,' he protested, pulling away from her.

The eagle raced past overhead, glancing down at them,

screeching its warning, its eyes wild with terror as the silent cloud followed. Sari pulled Perak along against his will. Turning back to check on the others, she saw the dark cloud dip towards them. A glimpse of electric green flashed from underneath as it approached. Raden's shadow fox ran in circles, panting and whining as he ran. Sari ran.

Netro called out to her. 'Sari, it's butterflies! Look at them; they're as long as my arm.'

Sari turned back. 'Perak, he's right, it's only butterflies, oh they are so beautiful, how I pray for a shadow butterfly.'

She became captivated by the powerful flight of what she guessed were at least twenty giant butterflies. Netro had not exaggerated their wingspan, which was nearing half her height. Their size did not spoil their flight. They seemed to skip gracefully on air. Their powerful hind and forewings fluttered the colour of night. Luminous green triangles posed in neat rows against the black of each wing. They glided and fluttered. Sari suspected they knew precisely where they were going. Each flutter seemed to be timed in unison, and they flew with precise control. As they got closer, Sari became alarmed by their large black claws, which tucked neatly into their red, furry bodies. The eagle was now forgotten. The hairs on Sari's arms stood on end as the giant butterflies folded back their wings and dived down towards them. Raden's shadow fox darted past Sari and Perak, heading for the safety of the trees. Raden's fox looked back for a moment and barked wildly at Raden, who seemed determined not to follow. The black mass raced overhead, creating a shadow over Raden and Netro. Sari suppressed a cry of fear as the shadow raced toward them and hovered over Sari and Perak.

The butterflies had set their course on Raden's shadows fox. Dipping lower, the chase began. They increased their speed to catch the fox as he scurried for the trees. He had nearly made it.

'Run Shadow, run,' yelled Raden.

The fox seemed to hesitate, not understanding his master's words. The butterfly's shadow covered him. He flattened himself in the long grass as they swooped down upon him, enveloping him in their mass of fluttering wings. Sari could no longer see him, but the growling and yelping from under the wings frightened her. Raden and Netro charged past her with their machetes held high.

They released their battle cry. 'Protect those created by the goddess.'

Sari restrained Perak by the shoulder, unsure what to do.

Perak pulled away. 'Come on,' he insisted.

She lurched forward, her small knife waving in front of her with her heart hammering in her chest as she caught up with Perak. She saw the boys hacking into the wings of the outside-ring of butterflies, which surrounded the fox. The butterflies fluttered around to face their attackers, their claws swiping in defence. She hesitated as she watched Perak take his first victim. Two butterflies rushed towards Sari, and she stabbed her knife through the air connecting with the green triangles of one of her enemy's wings. Unbalanced, it wobbled and crashed to the ground. Struggling on its back, its evil black eyes glazed over in defeat. The other butterfly attacked her from behind, its long tarsal claws striking the top of her head. She screamed in horror. Perak stabbed at its wings with his small knife, severing one wing from its body. As it toppled over backward, its antennae quivered with the last of its life. Sari lunged forward and thrust her knife into another fallen butterfly's striped red body. Its claws scratched at her arms, bringing Sari to her knees. Perak thrust his blade between the butterfly's eyes, ending its life. They worked together.

Netro called out to them. 'Help us, Sari, Perak.'

Perak pulled Sari to her feet, and they entered another fray of butterfly wings. Sari's scream turned into a roar as they charged forward with their knives held high above their heads. Netro and Raden each had a butterfly attacking them. Sari positioned herself next to Netro, and Perak went to Raden's side. She lunged forward and sliced off the butterfly's antennae with one swoop of her knife through the air. It turned and took a swipe at her with its claw. She jumped back. With its underbody exposed, Netro slashed his blade down the length of its body, spilling its guts onto the grass. Sari distractedly poked the foul-smelling contents with her knife. Netro roared, bringing her back to her senses. Raden and Perak were holding off two larger butterflies that beat their mighty wings in their faces, knocking Perak to the ground. Sari stared at the pulsing blue veins on the underside of its wings. She got a glimpse of what they were protecting behind them; their Queen. The queen was much smaller than her protectors, but with very similar markings except for her gold-tipped wings. She perched on the shadow fox's back as he lay on his side, her long proboscis uncoiled as she sipped the blood of Raden's shadow fox delicately through it. Sari boiled with rage. The Queen turned her eyes on Sari. Sari stared back at her through the wings of her protectors.

'You, you un-goddess creature,' she spat.

The Queen slowly coiled up its proboscis, its eyes never leaving Saris.

'Go, or you will meet your maker,' Sari roared.

She saw a small gap between the fluttering wings of the Queen's protectors and dived beneath it, landing face-first in the grass in front of the Queen. Ducking to avoid a swipe of Raden's knife, Sari quickly got to her feet and faced her rival. The boys stabbed furiously at anything that moved. The Queen unhooked her claws from the shadow fox's back as

Sari lunged toward her. Sari flailed the air with her knife, missing. The Queen began to rise into the air, fluttering delicately. Sari stabbed again, connecting this time with one of the Queen's gold-tipped wings, making a clean tear. It flapped in the breeze. The only sounds came from Sari as she snarled and stabbed at the air. The Queen fluttered out of her reach. The remaining butterflies darted quickly upward to meet the Queen. They fluttered just out of Sari's reach, then turned and soared away. Sari watched for a moment, her anger on the surface.

Raden stumbled towards his fox. His shadow fox lay panting quietly on its side, surrounded by injured and dying butterflies. Netro and Perak kicked the surrounding butterflies to the side, clearing their way. Sari joined the boys, and they gathered around the fox, coming to their knees beside Raden. Deep claw marks ran down his back, blood matted his brown fur.

'Nothing can be done. We should go before they come back.' Raden's voice made Sari's heart squeeze.

'We can't leave him here,' Sari whispered, looking around at the company he kept.

'He wants us to go. That is the way of the shadow fox. If he could, he would go off into the forest and die alone.'

'Well then, at least let's carry him to the trees.'

Raden silently agreed, picking his fox up and heading to the trees. Sari looked at her brothers. They were also covered in blood, which oozed from deep scratches. Her head throbbed. They followed Raden and watched him as he placed his fox next to a large tree.

'Goodbye, my friend, guide me in spirit.' He turned and walked away. His back was rigid, his face pale.

Sari knelt beside the fox, stroking his head gently. 'May the goddess watch over you. Thank you for saving us.' Sari knew he had saved their lives by diverting attention away from them even though it had been in fear, she thought.

Sari caught up to Raden. She took his hand in hers and walked quietly next to him for a while along the tree line. Once they felt they were a respectful distance away, they sat and tended to each other's wounds. Most of the scratches were superficial wounds, but Raden had a very deep injury to his underarm. Sari decided she needed to stitch it. She took out her wooden needle and threaded it with a fine twine from her kit.

'Ready?' she asked. Her hand shook, she had never sewn flesh before.

'Yes.'

'I'm sorry.'

'You will do fine, just trust yourself,' Raden said gently.

She couldn't bear to add to the pain already clear on Raden's face, but the wound could not wait for her. She pushed the needle through his skin and began to stitch. She felt his body tense. She hesitated.

'Keep going,' he encouraged, through gritted teeth.

She decided not to look at his face and sewed quickly. Snapping the twine after knotting it, she then bandaged it tightly with a long strip of cloth.

'There, all done,' she announced proudly.

'Thank you.'

Netro had been helping Perak with his wounds, and Sari inspected her brothers' wounds. Netro then wiped the blood from her head and arms.

Too exhausted to talk, they didn't speak about what had happened.

'We should keep moving. It's not long until sunset, and we need somewhere to sleep,' Netro said, taking over from Raden, who sat silent.

Sari was now very afraid. Their adventure had turned

sour, and she wanted to go home. Sari took a long look at the trees on the other side of the clearing. She was too afraid to go back in case the butterflies returned, so she reluctantly moved forward with the others. Sari studied Raden's hunched shoulders. *It was very bad luck for your shadow to die.*

Rubbing her necklace, she sent up a silent prayer and cursed herself for believing in such nonsense.

4

VILLAGE DEAL

They walked in single file, silent, but watchful. The leaves, now dry, crunched beneath their feet. Sari's ears strained at every sound. *Giant butterflies... what could have caused this? Was it normal?* Sari wished her papa were here; he would know the answers. They stumbled across a natural pathway which they followed for ease and because it more or less went in the direction they were headed. Sari heard running water, and they soon found themselves walking along a narrow stream leading to a small waterfall. They refilled their water flasks and took a break. The sun goddess shone high overhead as Sari squinted at her. She looked back at the small waterfall and watched its spray of fine mist catch the rays of the sun. The forest was as beautiful as Sari had imagined. She had seen sketches in books, but no book could bring to life the beauty before her. She tried to push the butterflies from her mind, but they hung there, crowding her thoughts.

'Let's keep going,' she said.

They consulted their map once more, and Sari took the lead following the stream. The boys lumbered behind her.

They came to another clearing with a large lake in its centre.

'Which way?'

They gathered to consult the map.

'Wait; something's not right look at that, the water has stopped flowing into the lake.' Netro squatted down, touching the hard surface. 'It's cold, looks frozen.'

'It's purple, purple ice,' Sari said, astonished.

Sari looked up at the sun goddess, whose golden rays beat down upon the lake, seeming to have no effect. She watched the water from the stream trickle down and freeze on impact as it hit the body of the lake.

'How can this be?' she said, squatting next to Netro, touching the purple glaze.

'You have to admit it looks beautiful.'

'Yes, so did the butterflies,' said Raden.

She got up abruptly. 'Let's just get away from here.'

I don't like this,' Perak moaned.

'What's the hurry? Let's look around. We need to see what has happened here,' Netro said, unconcerned by a frozen lake in the middle of goddess season.

'I'm getting the same feeling I had at the last clearing,' Raden urged.

Sari didn't need to be reminded. She grabbed Perak's hand and quickly followed him to the right, sticking close to the frozen water's edge as they walked around it. Netro followed reluctantly. Every so often, they would stop and stare at a lifeless bloated fish staring up at them from under the thick ice; its glassy eyes frozen in terror.

'Looks as though they've been poisoned by this purple stuff,' Netro said.

They ignored him and walked quickly. Sari felt relief wash over her as they reached the other side of the lake. Her new mission was to put the frozen lake behind her.

SELENA JANE

They stumbled back into the forest where the stream began to flow freely once more.

Netro pointed. 'Look at that, the water is clear and flowing again as if nothing had happened.'

'Yeah, just like the butterflies disappearing,' Raden said sarcastically.

'Okay, let's just keep walking and pretend none of this is happening,' Netro snapped.

'Okay, Netro, leave it alone; that's enough. We are all tired,' Sari implored.

Netro narrowed his eyes.

Sari felt weary and struggled to keep up with the boys as they walked along the stream. An eagle screeching overhead quickened their steps, their feet squelched through red mud. Insects glided on the water beside them, and Sari monitored her ankles, making sure no uninvited guests were helping themselves to her blood. The stream widened and pooled into another small lake.

'We can set up here for the night,' Raden decided, dropping his sack.

Sari wasn't happy about sleeping by the stream; she knew she would be eaten alive by bugs. She looked at Raden's wound and the strain on his face and knew he couldn't go on. She placed her straw mat by an old tree. The group ate little, and they barely spoke.

Once Raden and Netro appeared to be asleep, Perak came over to Sari's mat and lay down beside her.

'Have you ever heard of giant butterflies before?' he whispered.

'No,' she answered quietly.

'What about frozen lakes in the middle of goddess season?'

'No.'

They lay silently, listening to the breep, breeping of tree frogs.

'You were very brave, Perak. Thank you for helping me. Papa would have been proud of you.'

'Do you really think so?' Perak's voice twanged with pride.

'I'm sure of it.' She ran her fingers through his curls. 'Forgive me, I was wrong, you are old enough to come on this journey with us, although I expect you would rather have stayed at home now, considering...'

'Are you crazy? I wouldn't have missed this for all the figs in Elok Beach.'

She smiled in the moonlight, shaking her head.

* * *

The morning brought a map of bites to Sari's skin.

Raden swiped her busy hand away from her legs. 'Stop scratching, Sari.'

'It was your idea to camp here.'

'I'm sorry. I wasn't thinking.'

Looking into Raden's sad eyes, Sari immediately felt guilty. 'It's okay, they're not too bad,' she lied.

Netro kept to himself. Sari wished she were closer to him, so she could get inside his head. She suspected he felt sad for his friend and perhaps even questioned his own motives for coming on this journey. She soon realised she had been wrong about her brother's feelings when he finally spoke.

'This is the greatest adventure! I need to find out what is happening here. Maybe the Holy Whale has something to do with this.'

'You can't be serious?' she asked.

'Our village is not the only one with problems, giant

butterflies, frozen lakes. There's some imbalance in nature here.'

Sari glared at him.

'What?' he said, frowning.

She nodded towards Raden, who sat staring into the forest.

Netro shrugged.

That's it, she thought, she was convinced her brother had no regard for anyone but himself. She couldn't believe they were even related.

* * *

They followed the stream for most of the day. It became very narrow at points and then widened again. They decided to have a dip while the sun goddess hung high in the sky. Sari felt cautious about getting into the water but was comforted by the fact that it was a very narrow stream. It couldn't possibly house anything terribly big, she thought.

The boys stood in the centre of the stream splashing one another.

'Come on in Sari,' they cajoled.

'How do you know it's safe?' she called.

Netro spat into the stream. 'See how my spit separates? The water is clear and running freely.'

Sari hid her irritation and joined them. Walking into the cold water, she closed her eyes, letting the water lap over her ankles and sat down at the water's edge, the water rising to her waist. She watched the boys splash one another. Raden turned away from the splashes, trying to keep his bandage dry, which soon became soaked through. He started back to the water's edge to take it off.

'A little sun will do it well,' he called, smiling for the first time since they had left his fox.

Sari's eyes fixed on a large and slimy, purplish-blue blob on Raden's thigh. Jumping to her feet, she yelled, 'Oh my, leeches! Purple leeches! Get out.'

Her brothers ignored her until they saw the leeches on Raden's torso as he exited the water. They were three times the size of any leech they had seen before and the colour of blueberries. They scrambled toward the bank. Raden slapped at the leech on his thigh. There were two more leeches on the backs of his legs, sucking away happily. Sari was leech-free, but her brothers each had several leeches on his legs and torso. The leeches grew bigger as they filled with their host's blood, their slimy purple bodies glinting in the sunlight. Perak hopped furiously on one foot and ran in circles as if chasing his own tail. The leeches continued to suck away, unperturbed by slapping hands. Sari tried to prise them off with a stick, but they held on tight.

'You'll have to burn them off,' Raden shouted above the chaos.

Between them, they lit a fire. Sari thrust the stick into the flames until its tip glowed red. Shaking, she pierced the red-hot tip of the stick into the fleshy head of a fat leech sucking on Perak's stomach. It dropped to the ground, squealing in agony, and Sari flicked the leech into the fire with satisfaction. She put the stick back into the flames and pierced her next victim. Sari repeated the process until every leech had been scorched and had been deposited into the hot flames. She looked at her boys, their bodies streaked with blood, and again found herself tending to fresh wounds.

She stayed calm, but when she finished, she cursed out loud. 'Goddess forsaken land!'

What was the point of cursing? It was already cursed! The

elders were right. They should never have come here, she thought as she marched off into the forest.

'Hey, where are you going?' Netro called after her.

'I'm going to do my business, why do you care?' she said, throwing her head back and leaving them behind her.

She walked some distance away, and as she crouched, she collected her thoughts. She watched hundreds of termites busily chomp through a fallen tree trunk and thought about the forest and how it provided for all of the goddess's creatures. As her racing heart slowed, she realised Netro was right; they needed to continue on and find out what was going on. She got up, took out her small knife, and calved her name in the nearest tree. Singing softly to herself, she smiled. Singing was something her mother would do when she felt anxious. Although the boys had not come looking for her, she realised she had been gone for quite some time and decided she'd better get back to them.

When she returned, she couldn't see them and knew instantly that they must be playing a trick on her. 'Okay, it's not funny. Come on out. We should get going soon.'

Silence.

'Come on, don't be silly,' she chided.

There was still no response, and she started to feel a little uncomfortable. 'Okay, you've had your fun.' Silence except a few birds twittering up high in the trees. She felt herself getting annoyed, and her stomach churned.

'It's not funny. Now come out right away, or I won't talk to you ever again.'

Her eyes searched the trees. Her lip began to tremble. She walked forward and saw what looked like drag marks in the soil, and her eyes brimmed over with tears.

She crouched, touching the marks in the dirt. 'Netro,' she whispered. 'Perak, Raden?'

She stayed crouched like this as time passed. Her head

whirled. She imagined the boys jumping out of the trees and saw herself reprimanding them as they laughed. After a time, she realised they were not coming back, and something terrible must have happened. She cursed herself for leaving them and acting so immaturely. *Okay! Get it together. You must follow the tracks. What did Grandpapa teach you about tracking? Put all your senses on high alert.*

She found the drag marks just before the grass began again. She breathed deeply through her nose. No, she couldn't smell anything out of the ordinary. *Listen!* She closed her eyes and listened hard, trying to block out the everyday forest sounds, searching for something different. She heard the faint sound of a horn blowing in the distance, but not too far away. *Good! Is the sound in the same direction as the drag marks? Yes!* The drag marks were only two feet long, and then the tracks were lost into the grass. She carefully inspected the grass. The blades were broken and bent to the right, indicating they had gone that way. *Remember*, she thought, *they might try to fool you. Be sure.*

She double-checked around her, but there were no other obvious indicators. She remembered their belongings and looked around to find that their packs had been taken. She had no supplies. Sighing deeply, she realised she was all alone with no food or water, and she felt slightly irritated about her grass mat. She checked herself, realising her brothers could be in danger. Crouching low, she took off to the right.

Sari frequently stopped to look at broken or disturbed vegetation. She realised they either didn't know she followed them or just didn't care. There were no sandal marks to indicate the boys, but plenty of footprints where the grass thinned out. The prints were of bare feet. Their indentations were quite deep, and they took short strides, indicating they were carrying something heavy. She figured out that they must have been carrying the boys somehow.

They were not running, as the prints were no deeper at the toe. The tracks were very fresh now, and she realised she might come upon them soon. She decided she had time to work out how many there were of them. She crouched and studied a fresh group of prints. They had similar sized feet, which made it difficult. Their feet were small. *Were they women? Hard to tell! Maybe men with little feet!* One thing Sari knew; they were not her people. She looked at her own narrow feet. Her brothers had slightly wider feet, but these prints before her were very broad at the toes and the toes were short and fat compared to her own slender ones. Sari became excited when she realised that one of them had lost a toe. Now she knew there were at least two of them. Sari studied the prints repeatedly, looking for differences, but could find very little to be sure of. She began to panic as time slipped away, and she lost her confidence. Sari closed her eyes and took a deep breath as Grandpapa had told her to do in these situations. She listened again and heard the faint blast of a horn and moved forward once more until she came to a stream. When she crossed to the other side, the tracks were lost.

She looked up and down the stream. 'Oh, goddess above, they are walking in the stream!' she whispered. 'Which way?'

Listening for the horn again with her eyes closed, she looked toward the sound downstream. She had to believe her group belonged to the horns. She took off slowly downstream, wading in the ankle-deep water, looking for more clues by checking each bank as she went. The stream widened and deepen, making her job more difficult as she waded backward and forwards to check each bank. The water came up to her thighs. *Why would they keep walking in the water when they have a heavy load? Surely that would slow them down.* She decided she must have missed something and doubled back. Glad to be out of the water, she rechecked the banks. She heard her grandpapa's voice in her head. '*Go on child, you can do it.*'

Looking up at that moment, her eye caught the sun shining brightly on a giant spider's web spun between two trees. Its lower half had been torn through the middle, and it swayed slightly in the breeze. Sari smiled as she approached the bank covered in small rocks. Behind one of the rocks a clear print showed deep in the mud. The two tall trees acted like an entrance to the woods, and the group had gone through the trees. She found more evidence of their passing, and Sari was soon on their trail once more. She quickened her pace, knowing she had lost time. Their tracks meandered along the bank of the stream. After some time, the horn blowing became closer, and she breathed in deeply as she got her first smell of smoke. She kept the stream to her left. It ran wide and deep, and as the stream rounded the bend, a village came into view.

She crouched down low and thought about what move she would make next. She decided she should proceed under cover of darkness. The sun hung overhead in the early afternoon.

Okay, I need some food and some rest first. Then I'll watch them and make a plan. I need to know my enemy first. No point charging in and getting captured.

Then her mind drifted as the dark images took her to wild stories she had heard of boiling men in pots and terrible tortures.

'No, can't think of that now. Stick to the plan.' She realised she had spoken out aloud and covered her mouth. She slunk away into the forest to forage for berries. Her stomach grumbled its annoyance, and her heart fluttered with delight on finding some figs, her favourite fruit. She sat with her back against a large tree trunk, taking a bite of fig as she watched a line of ants march busily across her path. She leaned her head against the tree and rested her eyes, her ears still alert to the sounds of the forest.

It wasn't long before Sari felt restless. She got up and headed towards the perimeter of the village. The sky opened, and the rain poured down, pelting her with large raindrops. She ran through the forest, chose a large tree and climbed up to the highest branch where she positioned herself so she could watch the comings and goings of the village. Sari shivered in her wet tunic, as water dripped into her eyes from her hair.

In the fading light, Sari took in the thatched structures made of palm branches.

She saw a large fire burning in the centre of the village, unperturbed by the heavy rainfall. They were dark-skinned people, dressed in brightly coloured grass skirts. Some wore braids in their hair. It was hard to judge their height from above, but she picked out a few small children playing by the stream as the women collected water in pots and carried them toward the fire. It seemed to be a busy time of day, and Sari thought of her own village.

The rain stopped as suddenly as it had started. Sari couldn't see any men or her brothers, but she heard male voices coming from a large structure over to the left of the village. The opening faced the stream, away from her viewing. A child strayed too close to the hut, a woman smacked his bottom, and he howled as his mother dragged him back to the fire.

After watching the women for a while, Sari decided it was safe to get closer to the hut. The women were busy preparing the evening meal and seemed to stay clear of the structure. When Sari was sure they would not see her, she slid carefully down the tree's slippery bark and crept through the village towards the large hut.

Sari stood now at the back of the structure, her heart

pounding loudly in her ears. Her knees nearly went from under her upon hearing Netro's voice.

'We must be allowed to continue on our journey. Our village...' Netro's voice was cut off by a murmuring among the crowd.

A man raised his voice in a language foreign to Sari. She pressed her ear to the wall of palm branches and closed her eyes so she could hear more clearly.

She had a sense of someone behind her a moment before a hand closed over her mouth. Sari was dragged backward, kicking and clawing at the night air.

When she tired of struggling, the hand around her mouth relaxed a little. Sari allowed herself to be pushed to the ground next to the roaring fire. A dozen round black faces stared at her from the group of women. They encircled her, each holding their index finger to their mouths, indicating that she should be silent. The heat from the flames warmed her face as she watched a small boy run off toward the hut where the meeting of men was taking place. The noise in the hut fell silent. The double doors burst open, and two large men in loincloths ran toward the fire. Sari cowered further to the ground as they approached. An explosion of dialogue foreign to her began between the two men and the women. Sari allowed herself to be pulled to her feet and dragged to the hut by both her arms. The men burst back through the doors with her between them. She faced a large crowd of villagers and her throat tightened when she saw her brothers and Raden sitting on a mat in front of what appeared to be the chief of the tribe. Their feet and hands were bound, but Netro's grin told her they were unharmed. Perak, however, looked as though he were about to cry, and Raden's face was hard to read. The chief sat on a throne carved from wood. His large, round frame wedged into the seat, threatening to split the wooden arms.

Netro cleared his throat. 'Chief Sakima, this is my sister Sari. I guess she won't be going alone to do her business again.'

Sari didn't know what to do but gave a little curtsy and smiled weakly. A proud-looking man standing to the right of the chief's throne seemed to interpret Netro's words. Sari watched as Chief Sakima's face split in two, sharing a broad smile, his white teeth parting to let out a deep belly laugh. The other men in the hut followed his lead and roared with laughter. Sari, slightly embarrassed, laughed nervously along with her brothers. Through this, Sari noticed that although Raden smiled, he was not laughing. Their laughter died down, and they placed Sari beside Raden. They tied her hands and feet in the same way as the boys'. Her mood changed with this gesture, and she once again felt confused. Netro, who sat closest to Chief Sakima with Perak next to him, seemed to have taken the lead. Sari looked at Raden. She wondered why he was not speaking for them as their leader.

Netro straightened. 'Sari, I've been telling Chief Sakima about our journey to find the Great White Whale and about the strange things we have seen.' He smiled reassuringly.

Raden pressed his shoulder against Saris as Netro spoke. She felt comforted.

The chief spoke, and the proud man interpreted in a deep clear voice. 'We also have suffered many plagues and have seen some strange happenings. A tiger strolled into our village last week. Most of the villagers ran for the trees except for a small boy who had been left behind. The tiger came to him and lay down and rolled over before him.' The interpreter's nearly hairless eyebrows arched. 'The boy stroked the tiger's fur. The mother screamed and ran to the child, but the tiger stayed on his back, purring.'

Sari instinctively knew to stay quiet.

Raden whispered in her ear. 'The chief doesn't believe our

story. He thinks we are here to cause trouble. He didn't believe you were out there. Maybe now he has seen you...'

Netro continued, 'So you see Chief Sakima, we really do seek the Holy Whale, and this is our sister Sari.'

The chief replied through his interpreter. 'The chief wants to hear Sari's story.'

Sari babbled over quivering lips. 'It is true. We seek the whale and answers to our village's problems. Our village will not survive another season without some help.'

The chief rubbed his chin and narrowed his round eyes, staring at Sari. He turned to his interpreter, and they whispered between themselves.

'Chief Sakima has thought of a solution for all. He will let you continue if you agree to let four of his men go with you.'

Without consulting the others, Netro nodded. 'We should work together to solve this mystery and bring peace and balance to our tribes.'

Sari turned to Raden, noticing his sullen mood.

'What is going on, why is Netro talking like this, and why is he speaking as our leader?' she whispered.

'Netro and I agreed when we were captured that he would take over as our leader.'

'Why?'

He shrugged. 'Because we could both see my emotions were getting in the way of my thinking.'

She felt his unease and let it drop. She wasn't sure she was comfortable with Netro taking the lead, but what choice was there?

Chief Sakima gestured for his men to untie them, and with a wave of his hand he dismissed them. They were led to a small hut. There seemed to be a debate about whether they should place Sari in another shelter.

'She stays with us.' The fierceness in Raden's voice and

eyes told anyone observing that he wasn't about to let Sari be separated from them again.

Everyone fell silent.

'Is this your wife?' the interpreter asked.

'No,' Raden snapped.

Sari felt the colour rush to her face and a familiar stir in her stomach, which always accompanied any special attention from Raden.

There ensued some discussion, but eventually, Sakima's men let her join the boys in the hut. Once inside, she hugged them all, unobserved. Perak dissolved into tears, collapsing into her arms. Sari reminded herself that he was just a small boy who needed his mother. She became more determined in her resolve to find their parents as she held him.

'You look tired. Let me take him.' Raden took Perak from her arms as two tribal women entered their hut bearing bowls of spicy food for each of them and animal skins for blankets.

With Raden distracted, Sari pulled Netro aside. 'What is going on?' she muttered. 'Why are you now our leader?'

'It's between Raden and me.' He shrugged.

'Well, I'm not sure I'm comfortable with you being in charge. Why are you letting these people come with us?'

'What choice do we have? Either they come with us, or they won't let us go. And if you don't like me leading, then go home. You shouldn't have come anyway. If you hadn't come, Raden would probably still be our leader.'

'What are you talking about? It's not my fault his shadow died,' she murmured.

'Just let it drop.'

'No, I won't. Maybe you could talk to Raden and help him...'

'Open your eyes, Sari,' he snapped.

'That's enough Netro come and eat something, both of you. We have an early start,' Raden cut in.

Steam arose from the bowls of food, and they ate quickly. The blankets were warm, sending Sari into a deep but restless sleep with Perak nestled into the crook of her arm.

* * *

They set off again the next morning with fresh supplies weighing down their packs. The whole tribe had gathered to wish them well. They walked a long procession line of smiling faces. They presented Sari with gifts of necklaces, bracelets, and trinkets made from bones, teeth, twine, wood, and flowers. Sari looked toward the end of the line, where four men waited for them with Chief Sakima, bows and arrows slung casually over their dark-skinned shoulders. They seemed to Sari to be young and fit.

Baruti introduced himself first. Sari knew that the first to be introduced was the most respected. She recognised him as the proud man from the previous evening. His big, black, muscled thighs bulged from underneath his short loincloth.

'I am Baruti, I will be your interpreter.' He nodded sternly and thrust forward his palm in greeting. His eyes avoided hers. When they had each pressed their palm to Baruti's palm in greeting, he spoke again, introducing two others. 'This is Jahi, and this is Montsho.'

They were lean in stature and stood to attention with their dark trim torsos ready for action. 'They are equal in status and have a reputation as fierce warriors.'

Sari noticed that Jahi had a toe missing on his left foot and made the connection to the men she had tracked the day before. She received pleasant, but non-committal faces from them as she greeted them in turn.

Baruti nodded his head toward his third companion. 'This is Chuma. He will cook for us.'

Chuma pressed his palm to each of theirs gently and smiled. He had picked up one of their words and repeated it several times in greeting. 'Friend. Friend,' he said, laughing.

Sari liked him immediately. His rounded belly popped over the top of his loincloth, Sari guessed Chuma had been sampling too much of his own food. His legs, however, were slim and strong, and Sari knew he was by no means lazy.

* * *

*I*t had been decided that Netro and Baruti would be their joint leaders. Sari watched as their heads bowed together over the map. They re-entered the forest in assigned pairs. Side by side, Netro led with Baruti, followed by Raden and Jahi, then Perak and Montsho, and finally Sari with Chuma bringing up the rear. Sari felt happy about this arrangement, as Chuma seemed the least intimidating to her. She smiled once more at his round face and rounder belly and giggled at the thought of him sampling all the food. Chuma gestured for her to bury the many gifts she had received, and that weighed her down. The earth was wet and soft, and she hid them next to a huge old tree that looked as if it had lived there for twenty of Sari's lifetimes. She kept only one necklace, her favourite, which to her was simple, but had been carved from bone with great care.

'Be quick,' Baruti barked, and they all fell back into line.

They moved along at a rapid pace. The morning sun sucked the ground dry from the previous evening's storm, and the forest smelt sweet and clean. Jahi liked to sing. His sweet, low voice rumbled through the forest, and Sari found the sound soothing. The birds chattered high above in the trees. Ground creatures scurried, and everything seemed brighter. Sari felt renewed after her deep sleep the night before. Perak, however, slowed down as he tired. A discussion began among the tribesmen. Montsho, Perak's partner, thrust Perak's pack into Sari's arms. She took it, feeling a little bewildered. Raden turned and saw the exchange, and the group halted once more as he broke the line to join her. Baruti followed, speaking to his men. Jahi stopped singing abruptly; there was more interpreting.

'In our tribe, it is customary for women to carry the extra load,' Baruti huffed impatiently.

Sari suspected it annoyed him that the pace had yet again been interrupted.

'In our tribe, it is customary for the men to do the heavy lifting. It makes sense as we are built stronger.' Raden stared down at Baruti, with a defiant scowl on his face.

'This is your brother's fault. I wanted you next to me,' he said to Sari, taking Perak's pack from her.

'Thank you, Raden.' Her eyes scanned the other members of the group who stood staring.

Raden's face softened. 'Are you all right? I don't like you being up the back like this.'

'It's okay. Someone has to be,' she responded, embarrassed now.

He turned, glaring at Chuma. 'You scream like a cockatoo if this cook touches you.'

She felt herself blush. 'It's fine, really. He seems nice.'

Raden was acting strangely, Sari thought. She had never seen this side of him before. These people seemed to bother him a lot.

Raden went back to his place next to Jahi, who shot Sari a brief, but sympathetic smile; he patted Raden on the shoulder gently and started singing again. Chuma placed both his hands over his heart and rolled his eyes playfully.

Sari was a little confused at what Chuma was implying, and then she laughed.

'No, no!' She shook her head. 'Friends, like a brother.'

Chuma laughed, shaking his head, gesturing again once more with his hands on his heart.

Sari no longer cared for his silly banter; turning from him, she looked straight ahead. They didn't speak again until they had stopped for lunch by a stream. The group avoided all open clearings, walking through the dense forest all morning. It had been nice and cool, but Sari's skin was on fire from bites and scratches. After he had prepared a simple lunch of honey, nuts, and figs, Chuma wandered into the forest alone while everyone else rested. When he returned, he carried a pouch filled with fleshy leaves, seeds, and roots. Sari watched him curiously. He laid his bow and quiver of arrows next to him and took a small clay bowl from his sack. Pressing the seeds and crushing the roots with a rounded piece of wood, he mashed them all together with some water that he had collected from the stream. He approached Sari with his concoction, pointing to her legs. Before she understood what he was trying to show her, Raden was at her side.

'What are you doing? Get away from her,' he scolded.

Chuma gestured towards her legs again. Baruti joined them, and Chuma spoke to him quietly, looking down at his feet.

Baruti's deep booming voice cut through Sari. 'He wishes to help with her bites and scratches. He has made a potion which she must drink to take the itch away. The leaves will help with the swelling.'

Sari saw that Raden felt foolish.

Snatching the pouch of leaves and bowl of potion from Chuma, Raden scowled. 'I'll do it.'

'No. I'll do it.' Sari said snatching the leaves and bowl

from Raden. She turned to Chuma, smiling. 'You are very kind. Thank you.'

She drank the potion, flinching from its bitter taste, and stared at the pouch of leaves. Chuma took a leaf from her and split it open. He demonstrated how she should rub the sap onto her bites. She followed his instructions, wincing as the sap entered her open wounds. Sari then took out a pressed flower from her pack and gave it to Chuma. She had been collecting them and pressing them since they had started out, something her mother had shown her to do when she was a little girl.

'You are very kind,' she said again.

Chuma accepted the pressed flower and smiled, holding it to his heart.

'This means it will be a treasured gift.' Baruti interpreted and then walked away, picking up his belongings. It was time to move along.

5

KOMODO BITES

*S*ari wondered how much longer it would take to reach the other side of the island as the forest terrain changed, becoming less dense. The wider open spaces made her nervous, but the silence bothered her the most. In the denser forest, there had been a constant buzz and twittering of noise, produced by insects and birds high in the treetops. Remembering the butterflies at the last clearing, Sari shuddered, looking around uneasily at the mass of soil dunes, a barren space where trees used to be. She looked longingly at the tree line in the distance. The group ahead stopped, watching and listening. *Let's keep moving,* she thought. To her relief, they moved off again slowly to the sound of their crunching feet over dry dirt and rocks. Sari felt naked without the trees, noting only a few reeds poking out of the red-grainy earth. She stared at a set of large animal footprints in the sand to her left, near a grassy dune, and broke the line to investigate. Chuma followed her and as she crouched to look at the prints in the dirt, she felt Chuma crouch beside her.

'Large animal,' she said almost to herself, knowing he

could not understand her. 'See? Five toes with sharp claws.' She pointed, demonstrating with her five fingers.

'Komodo,' he said, looking around, his eyes popping.

'Too big for Komodo dragon.' Sari gestured, widening her arms.

He shrugged, looking puzzled. She felt a shiver run down her spine. Whatever it was, she didn't want to be around when it came back. She was about to turn away, when she heard a very loud hiss coming from the other side of the dune. The beast scurried to the top of the sand dune, causing Sari to fall backward, taking Chuma down with her. The lizard stood on its hind legs, clawing the air, its long yellow, forked tongue hissing and flickering.

'Komodo,' Chuma repeated in a daze.

Sari's body froze as if she were under the purple ice, her eyes focusing on the Komodo's large jaw, which displayed rows of razor-sharp teeth. After its show of aggression, the huge lizard came down onto all fours, its long tail whipping from side to side, spraying dirt on the slight breeze. The Komodo readied for attack. Sari didn't see the arrow pierce the lizard's hind leg, but the beast turned in the arrow's direction. The Komodo ripped the shaft from its hind leg with its powerful jaw and lunged forward toward a new scent. Sari and Chuma ran for the cover of the trees. The Komodo scuttled toward the others who lay in wait in the grass on the opposing bank. Arrows whizzed overhead now that Sari and Chuma were undercover. Chuma squatted, took an arrow from his quiver and aimed, the arrow taking flight. Sari helped by handing the arrows to him as he fired arrow after arrow. Nothing slowed the Komodo lizard; not even the sharp arrows piercing his leathery blue-grey skin. Sari saw he was almost upon the group, and still he did not show any signs of weakening. She watched in horror as the men and her boys jumped up from their lying positions in the grass and turned to flee. She screamed and shouted, trying to distract the lizard's attention away from them, but it was too late. The Komodo had its target in sight.

Rushing forward and lunging toward its victim, the Komodo clawed him to the ground, making long deep scratches in his back. The giant lizard pinned him down between his massive claws. Sari could not see who went down with the lizard blocking her view from behind. She screamed and ran forward as the lizard's great teeth ripped into the man's shoulder.

Sari ran ahead with Chuma, who squatted every few paces and fired arrows into the lizard's back. The group on the other side of the clearing turned and ran back toward their fallen comrade. The Komodo, now injured and surrounded, hissed loudly as it stood over its victim, who lay quietly on his side. Sari released a scream of fury as the group continued to fire arrows into the Komodo's leathery skin. The group joined Sari in her shouting. The Komodo released his hold on the man as an arrow from Montsho's bow pierced its furrowed neck, blood spurting from the wound. With arrows tipped with red-brown feathers swaying in his blue-grey hide, the Komodo staggered toward the safety of the dunes. They let him go and rushed toward their injured friend.

Perak fell into her arms as Sari and Chuma dropped to the ground next to Jahi who lay still on his side in the grainy dirt, eyes open, staring. Chuma tore strips from his clothes, barking orders to Montsho and Baruti. He dressed Jahi's wounds, stemming the flow of blood. The men jumped to Chuma's orders, Sari realised he was not only their cook but their carer and equally important when it came to their survival. She tried to help by cradling Jahi's head in her lap. She looked into his eyes. He had not made a sound. His dark face contorted in pain, yet he uttered no words.

'You okay?' she said, hugging Perak.

He nodded; his eyes wide with fear.

They watched Chuma march into the grassland as Baruti barked at his departing back, signalling for Montsho to join him.

Baruti turned to Sari and glared. 'No one goes alone.'

Sari felt the blood rush to her face as she looked down at Jahi's contorted features. 'He must be in so much pain, yet he is so quiet, he must be in shock,' she whispered.

'It is the way of our people,' Baruti answered more softly. 'We do not show our suffering, and we must die with dignity.'

'But he's not going to die! Don't say such a thing. Chuma will make some medicine for his pain and he'll get better.'

'I have never seen a Komodo as big as that before, and the dragon's bite will cause his blood to poison. He will die soon,' Baruti said, with no emotion in his voice.

She shook her head. 'You must be wrong. I remember a man from our village was bitten once, and he survived. With rest, care, and medicine, he'll be fine, isn't that right, Raden?'

Raden looked at her solemnly. 'Yes, Sari, you are right, but that dragon was small, nothing like this one.'

She wanted to cover Perak's ears to hide this awful truth.

'Come, Netro,' Baruti spat. 'We need to keep moving. We must decide what to do.'

Netro and Baruti walked a short distance away.

'We must decide what to do,' Sari mimicked, pulling a face.

She caught snippets of their conversation as darkness fell, and Sari could feel the terror coursing through her body at the thought the lizard would come back. She wanted to get moving, but she was determined not to leave anyone behind, and they could not move Jahi. She prayed that Netro would do the right thing and stand up for their beliefs as a family. After some heated discussion, their voices died down. Sari noticed that Baruti had the final word, but she felt relieved that they had come to an agreement.

Raden lit a fire. 'This will keep the Komodo away.'

Sari sat quietly with Perak and Raden still cradling Jahi's head in her lap, and she sang softly to him. It was the only thing she knew about him; that he liked music. They spoke very little. Raden sat close to Sari, and she felt comforted by the slight touch of his arm next to hers. Forest eyes stared at them through the trees. Shuddering, she wondered to whom they belonged. Chuma came back with his pouch once again filled with what Sari hoped would cure Jahi. He put a clay pot half-filled with water onto the ready-made fire, adding bark, roots, various seeds, and a cut piece of vine from his pouch. He sat staring at the pot, waiting for it to boil, occasionally glancing at Jahi. Sari wished she had some words of comfort for Chuma. He stirred the pot, and then carefully drained off the water through some cloth into another bowl. Netro and Baruti re-joined them as Chuma mashed the stewed remains in the cloth, leaving a mushy paste. Sari's interest piqued as she watched him take a small pouch from his sack. Opening it, he showed her the powdery dust.

'What is that?' she asked.

Chuma spoke to Baruti, who interpreted. Sari wished she could have a private conversation without Baruti's input, but hid her annoyance.

'It is yam powder. Our medicine man gave it to him before we left. It is for healing,' Baruti said.

Chuma mixed a small amount into the paste and waited for it to cool. He undressed Jahi's wounds and applied the foul-smelling paste to Jahi's open cuts. The paste looked slimy, reminding Sari of the leeches at the lake. Chuma then redressed the wounds in strips from his pack and re-boiled the remaining water. He added the same leaves that he had used to rub on Sari's legs and sprinkled in a small amount of yam powder. Sari helped Jahi drink the watery green liquid, while it was still hot.

Netro came and sat with them, avoiding Jahi's eyes as he spoke. 'They want to leave him behind and keep going.' He held up his hand before Sari could speak. 'You know they are under the order of Chief Sakima.'

Sari shuddered, but said nothing under Baruti's watchful eye and continued to tilt the cup for Jahi.

'He is their man, so we must respect their wishes, but I told him that I am the leader of this tribe, and they must consider our customs,' said Netro.

Sari allowed herself a little smile.

Netro continued. 'They agreed to stay here for one night and send Montsho back to get help. If Montsho is not back by the morning, we leave without him and Jahi,' he said, throwing a stick into the fire.

'But that would leave Jahi alone and defenceless,' Sari said, trying to keep her tone light.

'Sari, Jahi might not survive the night. It's the best I could do.' Netro whispered, pleading with his eyes for her to understand.

'How will Montsho go all the way back to the tribe and back again by morning?' she asked. Shaking her head.

Baruti spoke. 'He is swift, and he will run. If he is not back in time, then it is the will of the forest.'

Baruti relayed their decision to his men as darkness enveloped them. Chuma prepared dinner, and Montsho ate quickly, readied his belongings, and disappeared into the night.

The night dragged for Sari and Chuma as they took turns in nursing Jahi through until dawn. When she slept, she dreamed of giant lizards and butterflies. Bloated fish stared up at her from under frozen lakes. Suddenly she was trapped under a frozen lake, and as she thrashed under the water trying to break the ice, she woke with Raden gently shaking her and cradling her head to his chest.

'Shush, shush, it's okay,' he soothed.

She allowed him to comfort her for a moment and then pulled away gently. 'I'm okay now, I'm sorry to frighten you.' She felt embarrassed.

'Don't be sorry, we have been through a lot.'

'How is he?'

He nodded his head toward Jahi's still form. 'He's still alive, but his breathing is very shallow.'

Chuma sat with his back to them, guarding Jahi. Sari got up and sat beside him, taking his hand in hers. Jahi's eyes remained closed, and they sat like that for a long time until Chuma gestured for Sari to go and lie down. She smiled weakly and moved back next to Raden, who had been sitting watching their exchange.

'You like this Chuma?'

'Yes, I trust him. He is a good man. I'll need to take your stitches out tomorrow.'

He nodded and they fell silent for a while. Raden cleared his throat.

'What is it, what's going on with you?' she asked softly as she lay down facing him.

He continued to sit up rigidly, staring ahead.

'Do you believe what the elders say, that one is doomed if their shadow dies before their lessons are learned?'

Sari felt shocked. Sometimes Raden said things like this, and it took her a moment to catch her breath.

'I don't know. It's what they taught us to believe.'

She thought for a moment, knowing she had been of no comfort to her friend as she struggled with her own beliefs.

'I do know that other tribes are living on this island and are not gifted shadows on their sixteenth season and yet they are alive and protected somehow. Your shadow is your guide, a side of yourself, but it is not who you are. Your spirit lives on in you, as does your shadow,' she said, shifting her hip on her mat.

Raden's eyes widened. 'You think so? What about the bad luck?'

'Make your own luck.' She smiled. 'Why have you decided not to lead? I'm not sure Netro is ready.'

He signed. 'I'm a loner, Sari. I'm not used to looking out for people and what with my shadow gone... well, I feel like, one minute I might just take off and leave you all here, and the next I want to kill anyone that comes near you. And anyway, Netro is the one that's the most passionate about this adventure. I'm just here hoping to find some lost relatives.' He smiled thinly.

'It will be all right,' she said.

She saw he felt a little better after her words and she felt pleased with herself for finally helping him. It seemed he was always helping her.

'Thank you, Sari. There is a lot on this island that we don't understand, and when we get back home, we will have lots of wild stories to tell. I can see the elders now... we shall spend the rest of our days in the punishment pits.'

They both laughed and then fell silent, feeling inappropriate as Jahi groaned behind them. Raden lay down next to her, their faces only inches apart. She felt his warm breath on her cheek as he whispered, 'get some sleep now; it will be light soon.'

* * *

Sari woke to the smell of breakfast as Chuma busied himself with organising the group. Sari remembered her dream; she had seen Raden's shadow fox running through the tall green grass. She decided not to tell Raden to not upset him again; besides, he was whistling this morning for the first time in days, as he helped to serve breakfast.

Netro brought her some food and sat with her. 'I hear you've had some bad dreams.'

'Yes, but some good ones too, I'm okay,' she said cautiously.

'I want to talk to you about Perak.'

'Yes?' she said, spooning a mixture' of maize and fruit into her mouth.

'I want to send him back to Sakima's tribe to wait for us there.'

'He won't agree to that, and I'm not sure I will either,' she mumbled through a mouthful of food.

Before she could say any more, he plunged on. 'You can go with him if you want. This is no longer an adventure, Sari, it's life and death, and it's dangerous. Raden and I have talked about this and he agrees that Perak should go back.'

'And me?' she whispered, looking over to where Raden sat.

'He believes you are safer with us. Being a girl, he doesn't trust that you will be safer with them.'

She continued to eat slowly now. How could she leave Perak? How could she not go on with Netro? Her mind swirled. She felt torn between her two brothers.

'Could Perak and I go on home with an escort?'

'It could happen, but I don't know what the elders will do. I mean, maybe it would be better if we all faced that part of the journey together. You will both be safe with Chief Sakima.'

Her mind raced. 'Let me think about it.'

'I need to know after breakfast. The others want to keep moving.'

'What about Jahi?' she said, looking over to Chuma who was helping Jahi to drink.

He got up and squeezed her shoulder before walking away. 'You know the deal. If Montsho has not returned with help, we will leave without him.'

With so much to consider, Sari's heart ached as she thought about what they must do. She finished her breakfast slowly as she carefully considered every option. Ultimately, she hoped to find her parents, and that helped her to make her final choice. The other tribe members had not yet returned, and it was almost time for them to leave. She checked on Jahi. One look at Chuma's face and she knew that not only did she have to go to find her parents, but her new friend Chuma would need her support.

Jahi looked gravely ill, and Sari wiped his brow for one last time. She regretted not knowing him better.

'I'll see you soon, but goodbye for now.'

She left him to find Netro.

Netro called his group together after hearing Sari's decision.

'Let me tell him. I have a way to make it sound good to him,' he said.

Sari put her arm around Perak as he sat down next to her, opposite Netro and Raden.

Netro got straight to the point. 'Perak, we need to leave soon, and you know help hasn't come yet. We need you to wait with Jahi until they get here.'

Sari glared at Netro. This was not what she had foreseen.

'It's a very important job. Can you do it and be brave?' Netro asked.

Perak puffed out his chest. 'I can do it.' He turned to Sari. 'I can, Sari, and then I can catch up to you. I'm a fast runner. Papa always said so.' He panted with excitement over his entrusted role.

Netro pushed on. 'Perak,' he said in an almost fatherly tone. 'You must wait with Jahi, sword at the ready and when the tribe members return you will help them take Jahi back to their tribe and wait for us there.'

'B-but,' Perak stammered. 'I want to come with you...'

'Perak, it is not safe for you.' Netro tried to take his brother's hand, but Perak pulled away, got up and stomped his foot in protest.

'It's not fair. You promised. I have fought well, and I haven't shown fear, and I have made no mistakes,' he pleaded, kicking the ground.

Sari jumped to her feet. 'I'm not leaving him by himself, Netro!'

Perak turned on her. 'So, you think I can't defend myself and Jahi?'

He turned to the others. 'She's just a girl, so why does she get to stay? She's no good to anyone.'

Sari winced.

Raden got up and stabbed Perak in the chest with his finger. 'Now listen to me; she is the eldest female in your family, and she has been caring for you since your parents...' He trailed off. 'Anyway, a little respect from you.'

'Sorry,' Perak sulked. 'But it's not fair,' he said, kicking the ground again.

'Sit down, we're attracting attention,' Sari pleaded.

'Perak, if our parents are...' He trailed off again. 'Well, you and I are the only ones left to carry on Papa's name.' Netro looked apologetically towards Sari. 'We must be separated in case something happens.'

Sari rolled her eyes. She thought Netro's reasoning very dramatic, but something seemed to stir in Perak, and he appeared to accept this logic.

'I will wait with Jahi, and I will wait for you with the tribe.' His face brightened. 'Maybe if you don't come back for a while I can come and save you.'

'Yes, that's a great idea,' they all agreed

Sari wondered whether Perak secretly hoped something would happen to them so he could do just that. She still felt uneasy about leaving Perak behind alone, but accepted that he would be safer with the tribe; only the goddess herself knew what was around the corner. She shuddered to think of it, but to leave him alone unsettled her. *What if the Komodo came back?*

When the time came to leave, she stalled as much as she could. Baruti became anxious and barked orders to anyone in his range.

Netro insisted, 'Sari, we need to go now.'

A faint horn blew in the distance. Baruti took out his horn, put it to his lips and returned the call with a single blast from his own horn.

'They are not too far now, and we must go.'

He turned to Perak. 'You are a brave young man,' he said, and marched off into the forest with Chuma at his heels.

Sari and Perak clung to each other.

'Promise to come back for me,' Perak whispered into her ear.

'I promise.'

Sari wept openly.

Netro pulled her away and with a final wave, he frog-marched her back into the forest on the other side of the clearing. She turned one last time to see Perak standing tall, his chest puffed out, with his sword in one hand, silent tears sliding down his dirty face.

* * *

Sari hacked lazily at the undergrowth around her feet. The knife felt cold in her hand. She looked up, realising the forest had become very dense, and the group hacked ferociously up ahead of her. She saw their sweat, and she saw the pain on their faces. She heard their groans, but for once she was wholly absorbed in her own feelings. She barely answered when anyone inquired after her. No, she didn't want to move up the line; she was happy bringing up the rear for once. Many times, she looked behind her, tempted to go back. They heard the horn again behind them. There were several short blasts and then silence. Baruti did not reply with his horn but explained that it was a signal from his men to say that they had arrived and all was well.

Sari shook with relief. 'Why do you not respond?' she wanted to know.

'It is not safe. Montsho will track us and will tell us what has happened.'

Sari decided that she didn't like Baruti. He was rude and abrupt. She was no longer sure who was in charge. Sari knew that she needed him to help her find her parents, or Raden's grandparents, or Netro's Holy Whale. Thinking of these things lifted her spirits slightly. She knew Perak would be safe and she needed to focus on their journey.

The morning flew by with Baruti and Netro taking the lead. They would stop briefly to consult the map, but they seemed to be heading straight ahead. No one had been through this part of the forest for a long time, in fact, even the small forest creatures seemed to have forsaken it. Sari had not seen a snake all morning. She'd seen no rodents either; in fact, she couldn't remember the last time she had seen a spider or any kind of insect. The birds still called overhead, so that was of some comfort, but she hadn't seen one, as they were too high up in the branches of the tall trees.

They finally stopped for lunch as the sun goddess looked down from high overhead. Baruti, Netro, and Raden hacked a circle for them to sit in, while Chuma readied their lunch. *Poor Chuma*, Sari thought. She had hardly acknowledged him all morning. She offered to help, and he gestured for her to sit down.

'Thank you.' She flopped down gratefully, and he smiled briefly, going back to his work.

To her surprise, Baruti walked over to her with her lunch and sat down next to her. She ate cautiously, waiting for him to talk.

'Tell me of this great white whale that you know of,' he said.

She swallowed hard, her eyes flicking to Netro. 'Oh, Netro can tell you about it all.'

'I have heard Netro's beliefs in this whale. I want to hear it from you.'

She shifted uncomfortably, looking to Netro again for support. When he didn't come to her rescue, she stammered, 'I can only tell you that my grandpapa would speak of this great white whale. He called it the Holy Whale, and he said it was all giving and all-powerful.'

She felt silly saying it out aloud and expected him to laugh at her as others had done when she was a little girl. The freedom to talk of such things felt strange to her. When Baruti didn't laugh, she went on. 'The legend says that the Holy Whale travelled the entire world bestowing blessings on the islands he visited, therefore giving good weather, calm tides, abundance in all things from the ocean, fresh fish, clear waters, clear skies, so many things.'

'And you believe that one whale can do all this?'

She faltered, feeling his disapproval. 'Well, no. I didn't say I believe; besides, there's more to it.'

'Why are you making this journey? It is dangerous times for a woman.'

She wasn't sure if she was angry at his question or embarrassed by him calling her a woman, but she stood up and glared at Baruti, her voice rising.

She waved her hand around her head. 'Well, maybe Netro didn't tell you, but we lost our parents in the last great wave, and maybe they could still be out there somewhere. Or maybe I'd like to stop whatever is causing these disasters to happen, so I don't lose anyone else.'

Baruti also got to his feet and turned to Netro. 'She can stay. She has a fire in her belly.'

In his native tongue, he instructed Chuma to pack their belongings.

She gave Netro a dirty look. 'What were you going to do? Send me back with Montsho's escort?'

Netro shrugged, muttering as he walked away, 'I'll tell you later.'

* * *

A loud cracking sounded from above. Sari stood frozen to the spot, looking upwards as a large tree came crashing through the forest rooftop. Someone pushed Sari, and she was thrown clear as the large trunk slammed into the ground, landing inches from her outstretched body. A cloud of dust enveloped her face, and she coughed and spluttered on a mouthful of forest floor debris.

When the dust settled, she found Baruti lying beside her. The rest of the group was left standing on the other side of the enormous tree trunk. They stood peering over the bark, relief clearly showing on their faces.

Baruti helped Sari to her feet.

'Thank you,' she said, dusting down her knees.

'You would have done the same for me.' He smirked.

She smiled weakly, feeling guilty, not sure that she would have helped him. *How one full moon can make a difference*, she thought. Her opinion of Baruti had changed once again.

6

MONKEY DIVE

*T*he day, long and hot, beat down. Raden hacked away slowly at the scrub just in front of Sari, the hard work being done up ahead of them. Sari felt jumpy after her close encounter with the tree and looked up frequently to the forest rooftop.

She questioned Raden. 'Do you believe we will get to see the Holy Whale?'

'Not really, but something is going on. Chief Sakima wouldn't have sent some of his men with us if he didn't believe it too. It has affected our people for many moons, but Sakima's people only noticed changes in the last season. Before you found us at their village, they talked of placid tigers, giant insects, dead fish in streams, and many other strange happenings.'

'If the Holy Whale is real, why do you think he deserted us? Are we bad people?' she said, pushing a long hanging vine out of her face.

Raden turned back to look at her. 'I don't think our people are bad, but there is a lot of division, confusion, and maybe the truth got lost somewhere along the way?'

She looked up ahead to where Netro and Baruti, their leaders, spoke in hushed tones.

Raden followed her gaze. 'At least our leaders seem to agree about something. I trust Netro, and if he trusts Baruti, then that's good enough for me.'

'I know, Raden, but Baruti confuses me,' she whispered.

'He'll grow on you I expect, just like Chuma is growing on me.'

They both turned to look at Chuma, and he rewarded them with a wide grin, his first smile of the day. It warmed Sari's heart, and she realised it was the first time all day that she hadn't been aching over Perak. They halted up ahead.

'What is it?' she asked, her heart hammering in her chest.

Netro gestured for them to join them up front. A pungent smell carried on the slight breeze stinging her nostrils. A monkey lay at Netro's feet. Sari couldn't see any blood on its black silver-tipped fur, but she knew the monkey was dead. She dropped to her knees, facing the monkey which lay on its side, with its knees tucked into its silver-white chest. Sari ran her fingers through its thick black fur. Swatting flies from the monkey's head, Sari revealed the delicate features of its dark-skinned face. Its large, round mud coloured eyes stared up at her with a look of surprise frozen in them. The monkey reminded her of her papa's shadow monkey, the same kind, but fully grown, about half the length of her arm. Sari studied its long, black slim fingers, which were curled into a fist. Her eyes travelled his hairy torso, down to his toes, not unlike her own except for the black toenails. She cried silently at first and then she began to sob. Raden sat down beside her and put his arm loosely around her shoulders.

When she had calmed a little, he spoke gently to her. 'Sari, you need to know there are others.'

She sighed and got up, following Raden through the maze

of bodies. Some of them lay on their backs with their long skinny legs splayed. A few lay curled on their sides like the first monkey. There were nine dead monkeys, including three babies. The mothers and babies bothered Sari's the most. She felt numb as she went from body to body, touching them silently. The boys' faces told her they too struggled with the baby monkeys.

'What could have caused this?' she asked Raden as he knuckled a tear from his eye.

'It looks as though they fell out of the trees,' he replied sadly.

'What, all of them? How could that happen? Have you ever heard of monkeys falling out of trees?'

'I know it happens sometimes, but not an entire family of monkeys at one time.' He sighed. 'But I can't understand why they would be here, so far from the beach or the mangrove swamps.'

'Maybe they sensed danger and fled, but I still don't understand why they would fall out of the trees,' she said.

'They probably ate something that made them sick,' Netro suggested.

'Yes, maybe. I'm glad Perak wasn't here to see this; he loved papa's shadow monkey,' she murmured. 'Let's get away from here.'

They continued on, leaving the stench and decay behind them. Sari heard a noise to her right.

'Shush, I think I hear something,' she said in a low voice.

They waited.

'I don't hear anything Sari,' said Netro.

She shook her head.' Sorry. I'm just jumpy.'

But something nagged at Sari to explore the area where she had heard the sound.

'We don't have time for this,' Baruti chided.

He stood rooted to the spot as Sari crouched near his feet, sweeping leaves from side to side.

Raden got down beside her, searching the undergrowth with her.

'What did it sound like?' Raden asked.

'Like a hiccupping,' she said. 'Be quiet.'

The others stood looking at each other.

'Sari, Baruti wants to get moving,' hissed Netro.

'Look who follows the rules now,' she snapped. 'He'll have to wait.'

'I must insist,' Baruti ordered.

'Just let her look. What harm can it do? It would help if you moved out of the way.' Raden scowled.

Baruti stood his ground. 'I am not moving until we are all moving together.'

They heard the hiccupping again.

'It's coming from behind you, move,' cried Raden, pushing Baruti out of the way, brushing some large foliage aside.

'Sari, look!'

She came to his side, looking down to where a bright orange baby monkey lay on its back, hiccupping quietly with its slim black finger up its shiny flat nose. The fire orange hair on its head and body contrasted with its small, dark-skinned face where large pleading eyes stared up at Sari. She took the baby monkey in her arms and turned to Baruti.

'You knew it was there. Why didn't you tell us?'

'Look at it; it's hungry. We have no way to feed it and no time to look after it. I make no apologies,' he said, glaring at her.

The baby monkey clung to her tunic, its hiccupping subsiding.

'Sari, give me a water pouch. I'll go back and see if I can extract some milk from one of the nursing mothers. There may be some milk still in their teats,' said Raden.

'We cannot waste any more time. This monkey is destined to die alongside its family,' Baruti grumbled.

Raden held up his hands. 'We cannot leave it to die, Baruti. It's not far, so keep moving, and I will catch up to you.'

'Then you must not go alone.' Baruti sighed, defeated.

'I'll go with you,' said Netro. 'Sari, you walk with Chuma.' Netro nodded to Chuma, who seemed to understand.

The monkey was very young. Sari stroked the orange spiked hair between its very large ears. When she turned to show Raden, he had already gone, and she stood alone with Chuma and Baruti, neither showing any interest in the monkey.

'Let us go now.' Baruti turned on his heel.

Sari followed, walking gingerly, protecting the baby from the bounce in her walk. It felt strange to be without her posse, but her new friend comforted Sari. Maybe the goddess would bless her with a shadow monkey. She decided she liked that idea a lot. The baby monkey took Sari's finger to its rubbery lips and began sucking it.

'Don't worry, baby, Raden will bring you some milk soon,' she soothed.

Chuma, seeing the exchange, took some paw-paw from his pack and handed a piece to Sari. She smiled and put it to the monkey's lips. The monkey's nostrils flared, and the hiccupping started again. Chuma shrugged. Netro and Raden caught up to them with a pouch only a quarter filled with mother's milk.

'There were four nursing mothers, so we got a little from each,' Raden said.

'It's not much, is it.' Sari sighed.

Netro frowned. 'Their milk dries up. Who knows, even this milk might be sour by now.'

'Gosh, I hope it doesn't make her sick.'

She held the pouch's spout to the monkey's lips. The baby gulped greedily. Netro, Raden, and Sari exchanged pleased looks.

'Save some,' said Raden.

When she pulled the spout away, the monkey grabbed for it, hiccupping once more.

'No more, no, baby,' she said. 'I'll rock you to sleep now so you won't think about food for a while.'

Baruti scoffed. 'You just delay its death.'

'We should start collecting shoots, young leaves, fruits, and seeds. We'll need to try a few things,' Raden said, choosing to ignore Baruti.

Sari rocked the monkey. Its eyes rolled and fluttered, fighting sleep.

'What will you call him?' whispered Raden.

'She's a she.' Sari smiled. 'And her name is Baby. Just Baby.'

Sari felt exhausted after the long walk. She wouldn't let anyone else carry Baby, and the monkey now felt like a dead weight in her arms.

'How much further, Baruti?' she asked.

'We will rest here tonight.'

'No, I meant how much further to the other side?'

He frowned, looking at the monkey in her arms. 'I was thinking two more nights.'

She ignored his disapproval; the excitement swelling inside her momentarily until the image of the dead monkeys flashed before her eyes.

* * *

Sari rolled out her straw mat as Chuma lit the fire. Turning her back on the others, she lay down under the half moonlight, thinking about the dead monkeys and cradling Baby tightly in her arms. She remembered her teachings and reminded herself to be grateful. She sent up a silent prayer of thanks that Perak was safe and that they were unharmed. She prayed to the sun goddess for a safe journey. *Could they really reach the other side of the island in two nights?* They had decided not to sleep in a clearing, and she felt comforted by the tall trees surrounding her. She wasn't hungry and drifted off to sleep.

Something woke her; her trained ear picking up on a noise; she looked down at Baby sleeping silently in her arms. She heard a swift and faint thudding coming from the same direction from which they had come. She sat up and looked around her in the darkness, as the fire burned low. The others seemed to be asleep, and she had missed dinner.

Rolling over, Baruti put his finger to his lips to silence her and got carefully to his feet, kicking Chuma to wake him. They stood, sharp daggers in hand. Sari placed her hand on her knife. Netro and Raden woke as Montsho came running swiftly down their newly made track. Baruti embraced him with such force Sari had to rethink her views on Baruti yet again. Baruti seemed genuinely happy and relieved to see him. Chuma served Montsho a meal, and Sari ate a little too. She couldn't believe that he had come so far so fast and had a million questions for him but waited patiently for him to eat first, eyeing him eagerly. Montsho cleared his throat and nodded at Sari, taking in the monkey in her arms. He spoke to Baruti with Baruti interpreting.

'Perak has gone back with the others. He was fearless. The Komodo did not return. Jahi is alive but very ill and has been taken back to the tribe. Chief Sakima sends no replacement for Jahi, and he approves that you continue. I am to return with your news.'

Sari thought she caught a look of dismay from Baruti. Perhaps he didn't like to be outnumbered, she thought. She realised that the conversation was over, and that was all the detail she would get. She lay down, again grateful that Perak was safe. They were soon all asleep.

Sari could only assume that Montsho had been given an update, for when she awoke he had already gone. She couldn't believe the stamina of these people. She felt tired and fed up. The forest seemed to become denser as they moved along throughout the morning. Sari noticed that a lot of the trees were covered in vines. They twisted tightly around their trunks, almost strangling them in their vice-like grip. As the morning slipped away, it seemed the vines were taking over the forest and hacking through them took extreme effort. Each time Sari cut into a vine, it oozed a bright orange gel matching the colour of Baby's hair. At first, she had felt sorry for the destruction she caused, but after a while, she realised that these vines were a threat to the trees and she took great pleasure in hacking away at them. Baby lay in a sling made by Raden and she carried her with greater ease. Sari noticed that the landscape climbed steadily, and the trees were thinning out once more. Sari looked up at the sun goddess. By the time she was fully overhead, the boys had consulted the map once more and they were in full ascent. The mountain didn't look too high from here, but Sari's calves burned as the climb became steeper.

'Let me take Baby,' Raden pleaded.

'I'm okay.'

They pushed through to the top before resting again. When the group finally reached its peak, it was flat and almost tree-free. It looked to Sari as if the top of the mountain had been sliced entirely off.

'It's like a tabletop,' Sari said in awe.

They walked for some time along the flat top, and Sari caught up with the others who stood staring over the face of the cliff. She stood next to Raden and stared ahead, panting slightly. She saw the ocean once more and smiled with relief. It drew her eyes to the beach where tiny dots; she presumed to be villagers were milling around village huts. Looking down over the cliff face, she dreaded the thought of climbing down, but saw no other way. There appeared to be more forest to trek through before reaching the beach. Her eyes rested there once more. As Sari watched the tiny dots with fascination, movement drew her eyes back to the water. *Shadows and lots of them*, she thought. They shifted and changed as she studied them.

She tugged on Raden's arm. 'Do you see the shadows in the water?'

'Yes,' he replied.

She tugged again. 'Do you think they are whales?'

'No, too many of them; must be sharks or some other creature of the deep. I guess we'll find out soon. Doesn't look too much farther; what do you think, Netro?' he asked.

'Baruti guesses one more night,' Netro said, cupping his hand to his forehead and peering ahead.

'And what do you think?' Sari said, feeling annoyed that her brother seemed to have lost his voice.

He didn't answer and continued to stare ahead, looking out to sea.

Chuma prepared a simple lunch of fruit and nuts, and Sari's stomach rumbled for more as she sat and listened to Baruti and Netro discuss their plans. She gave Baby the last of the milk and tried to tempt her with a few sweet fruits.

'We need to get there by nightfall, so we can spy on them,' Netro said.

* * *

95

*B*aruti carefully placed pieces of fruit on his tongue as if savouring each morsel. 'I agree, we should start out early tomorrow morning and arrive by nightfall. We will have the cover of the forest again just before we arrive.'

Sari lay on her side, yawning, supporting her head with her elbow. She hoped they would rest for the afternoon and relax, but her illusions were soon shattered with the next words to fall from Baruti's mouth.

'We should use the afternoon to ready ourselves for the journey ahead. We need fresh supplies, and our weapons need to be sharpened and repaired.'

Everyone seemed happy with the arrangement. Sari wondered if any of them were as tired as she was. She doubted it, but was too proud to let them know how exhausted she felt. The boys gave her the choice of either helping to sharpen arrows or gathering food with Chuma. She chose to go with Chuma, yearning to spend some quiet time alone with him. They had hardly communicated since Jahi's departure.

They walked together across the mountaintop away from the group. She caught Raden's look of concern and held up her hand to silence him. He let them go without a word, and she sighed to herself with relief.

The mountaintop offered very little in the way of food, and Sari followed Chuma back down the mountain slope, but in a different direction from that which they had come. They crept, with Chuma gently pushing through the light foliage ahead of her. Sari pulled gently on his arm. As he turned to her, she made a sad face and asked, 'Jahi?'

Chuma nodded and put his hand to his heart.

'He'll be fine now,' she said in a soft voice.

He seemed to understand and smiled. When they reached

the bottom once more, they walked back into the dense forest. Chuma's mood seemed to lift; he put his finger to his lips, pointing with his other finger above his head. Sari looked up. High in the tall trees she saw hundreds of fruit bats hanging sleepily upside down with their claws wrapped tightly around the tree branches. Chuma squatted down, positioning his bow diagonally across his body. He reached behind him, pulling a feathered arrow from his quiver, slung over his right shoulder. He placed the shaft snugly between the string and the curve of the bow and held his right thumb firmly under the string to keep the arrow in place.

Sari watched intently.

Chuma looked along the shaft of the arrow, aiming the arrow at his target above. He pulled the string and arrow backward gently and let the arrow fly with a twang. It soared directly upwards in a straight line, with feathers quivering as it pierced the bat's small body.

The bat released its grip and dropped out of the trees, landing with a thud at Sari's feet.

She looked at his small furry black body and his little pinched face. After a pang of guilt, she reminded herself they needed to eat.

'Well, that will not go around,' she said, showing the bat's smallness with her fingers, and Chuma laughed with delight.

He handed her his bow and an arrow from his quiver. She touched the tip of the arrow made from flint and found it was sharp. She adjusted the sling, so Baby wouldn't get in harm's way and, squatting down, she placed the shaft in the bow as he had shown her. She took aim; the arrow took flight, and it surprised her when the arrow stuck the first time, the tiny bat's body landing with a thud a little farther away.

Chuma chuckled with delight, and she burst out laughing. She quickly covered her mouth, worrying that the other bats would wake up, but nothing stirred them from their slumber. Sari felt relieved. She might feel awful if they woke up and saw their furry friends lying at her feet.

Chuma handed her another arrow, and she aimed again, striking another bat. They took turns in shooting, and she felt proud of herself, and she felt Chuma's approval as the tiny bats piled up at her feet. When they had collected fifteen bats, Chuma put them in his woven pack, and they continued on. They finally found some berries. They were red and sweet, and Sari had never had them before. Baby ate a few, staining the sling and Sari's tunic.

They dug up roots and collected shoots, all of which Sari carried in her pack. By the time they had finished, it was late afternoon. They had travelled far from the top of the mountain. Chuma made a fire and roasted the bats. Sari didn't question him as she knew it would not have been safe to light a fire on the top of the mountain. Once the bats were cooked and cold enough to carry, they ventured up the slope of the mountain. The hill was steeper on this route, but more direct with fewer trees. Chuma stopped to help Sari clamber over sharp boulders. He tried to take Baby from her, but she refused. Puffing, they reached the top, but still had to walk some distance along the flat top before reaching the others who had set up camp well away from the mountain's edge, roughly in the middle of the mountain's flat top.

Raden's face lit up on seeing her, and he scowled at Chuma. 'What took so long?'

Chuma replied by rolling out the bats in front of him. The others helped themselves to a bat, excited looks on their faces. Raden frowned.

'Here try one,' Sari said, trying to placate him.

Raden reluctantly picked up a bat and took a bite.

'We had to cook them first, and we have collected a lot of food for the journey,' she soothed.

'No reason to collect so much; we have always found food along the way,' he grumbled.

Sari shrugged. 'Don't ask me. I don't know.'

Baruti jumped in. 'Do not question what you know nothing of. I gave my man an order, and he followed it.'

Raden scowled. 'I'll question what I like. I was concerned for her safety. Next time don't send her off alone with strangers.'

'Calm down,' Netro mumbled through a mouthful of meat. 'The bats are tasty enough.'

Baruti spoke directly to Chuma, and they conversed for some time in their language.

Through Chuma's actions, it looked to Sari as though he were retelling their adventures of shooting the bats.

Baruti gave a rare smile and said, 'Raden, Chuma offers his apologies. I gave him orders to find food for the rest of the journey as he is not familiar with the coastline and is not confident of finding food in a strange land. I also ordered him to teach Sari how to shoot the bow and arrow as we taught you this afternoon. The only difference is, she shot something living, and you practised with targets.' He smirked.

'Did you shoot these bats, Sari?' Raden asked in astonishment.

'Maybe half of them.' She beamed.

Netro roared, 'A better shot than you, Raden.'

Raden laughed. 'It's windy up here, you know.'

Sari moved to the mountain's edge after dinner to watch the sun goddess end her day by sliding behind the ocean. Sari stood, taking a long drink from the water container. As Baruti approached, she turned to greet him, and he held out Montsho's bow.

'Chuma tells me you are a good shot. If you accept this bow and arrow you will fight with us if we need you,' Baruti stated formally.

'But this is Montsho's and you all believe it is bad luck for a woman to touch your bow or arrows,' she objected.

'We can wash it in sand and water when we get to the beach; that will be an excellent remedy for female interference,' he chuckled, handing it to her. 'Montsho made this himself and has had great success with it.'

She took the bow, tracing the delicate carvings with her finger. Green spirals had been painted on the surface of the wood.

'How did he make the green colour?' she asked.

'Green onions and tree sap. You will need his arrows too.'

He handed her Montsho's quiver containing six arrows as she laid the bow down next to her feet.

'The arrows are solid, made from witch hazel, and the feathers are from a brush turkey. You must try to look after it; it took a long time to make.'

'I don't know if I can use it,' she said.

'Was it easy to shoot the bats?' Baruti asked gently.

'Yes,' Sari noted his soft tone of voice and raised an eyebrow.

'Did you feel sad?' he asked.

'No, but that was different,' she said defensively.

'Why?'

'We were hungry, and I don't know anyone who has a bat as a shadow.'

'So, you needed to shoot it?' Baruti pushed.

'Yes,' she said

'Then you will shoot only when you really need to, and whatever it is you shoot at, it will be a bat to you in your mind.' He smiled.

Sari fell silent for a moment. 'Thank you, I will fight with you if you need me and I will use it wisely.'

Baruti nodded his approval. 'I see the monkey has taken

to fruit,' he said, acknowledging the monkey for the first time.

'Yes, I think maybe Baby isn't as young as we first thought.'

'Baby?'

'That's her name,' she said, her cheeks reddening under his stare.

'Tell me about these shadow animals, and why you don't have one. We do not have such a thing in our tribe.'

'We have a ceremony when you turn 16 summers. The stones are read by our wise woman, and she interprets the goddess's choice of shadow for you. It's a companion animal to teach you about what you are and what you are not.'

'I see. And you are not sixteen summers?'

She shook her head.

'Netro told me your papa's shadow was a monkey, is this why you became so upset?'

'Yes, we were all very attached to papa's monkey. Papa's shadow monkey taught us many things.'

'What happened to it?'

'When you have learned your lessons, your shadow dies or disappears, and we believe their spirit becomes one with yours, so you are complete.'

Baruti raised his eyebrows and was silent for a moment. 'Sari, when we get closer to the beach you should try to find a family of monkeys who will take her. You are becoming too attached.'

He strode away to join the others. Sari watched him walk away, fuming inside, but she knew he was right, and her heart lurched.

Raden came to sit with her, his torch flickering in the dimming light. Sari turned back to the ocean, sitting down and dangling her legs over the sharp cliff. Raden did the same.

SELENA JANE

'Beautiful isn't it.'

'Yes,' Raden agreed. 'Have you seen any more dark shapes in the water?'

'No, when I got here the sun goddess was already on her way down, so it was too dark to see.'

He handed her his knife. 'You promised to cut these stitches out.'

Oh yes, hold the light here,' she said, taking his blade as he offered her his arm and looked away.

She gently tugged on the stitches. The wound had healed cleanly, and she was happy with her handiwork.

'All done.'

He looked at her in surprise. 'Thank you. What was all that about with the bow and arrow before?' he asked as he rubbed Baby's fur between her rubbery ears.

'He wants me to fight with them if I'm needed,' she said, deciding not to share the discussion about shadows in case it upset him.

He nodded. 'Let's hope it doesn't come to that; either way, I will look out for you, Sari,' he said sincerely.

She felt herself blushing under his intent gaze.

Netro joined them. 'Tomorrow is when all our dreams come true,' he said as he plopped down next to her, giving her shoulder a brief, rough hug, causing her head to wobble on her shoulders. 'I will bring back hope and answers to our tribe and you will both...' He trailed off.

'You don't believe they are still alive, do you?' Sari said, shocked it hadn't occurred to her before that Netro thought their parents were dead.

'Sari, there is always hope, while it lives in your heart, and that's all that matters,' Raden interjected.

'But he doesn't believe it,' she said, holding Baby closer to her slim waist.

Netro ran his fingers through his dirty hair. 'It doesn't

matter what I think. As Raden likes to say, we each have our own destiny. Mine is to help our village, yours is to find answers to our parents' disappearance, and Raden's is to find answers about his family.'

Sari looked at Raden for support. She knew that this is what had bonded her so tightly to him. His desire was close to hers, and she knew he understood how she felt.

'So, your destiny is more important. Is that what you are saying?' she said, feeling annoyed with Netro once more.

'No, I didn't say that. Our destinies are all linked in some way, and each is as important as the other,' he assured her.

She let it drop. She would never understand what she saw as Netro's need for recognition and adoration. She got to her feet slowly, adjusting Baby's sling.

'Let's get some sleep. Baruti wants to head out before sunrise, and it's a long way down,' she said, trying to hide her disappointment.

7

CAPTURED HEARTS

*M*ist clung to them as they spiralled their way down the mountain's rocky path. Sari dared to peek over the ledge into the misty darkness before flattening her back against the cliff wall. Shivering as much from the cold as from the thought of plunging into the blackness below, she hugged Baby who looked up at her with eyes wide and frightened. Sari heard a large waterfall crashing against the rocks below her feet. They followed the track, descending into the valley.

* * *

*S*ari stumbled several times over rocks and large roots, which gripped the mountain's edge. Raden steadied her each time. The noise of the waterfall grew louder. Upon rounding the mountain they were met with a river of cascading water, which fell over the mountain into the valley below. The mouldy smell stung Sari's nostrils. The track became wet, and they slipped over moss-covered stones, which led behind the falls. The water hissed and crashed, spraying a fine mist over Sari's face. They stopped in the middle of the waterfall and looked out through the water's curtain, down into the valley, toward the ocean and the rising sun. Sari's nerves had been attacking her on and off all morning, and she felt pleased that they would follow the waterfall downstream as the water calmed her.

When they reached the other side of the waterfall, Baruti led them down through the forest, slightly away from the waterfall where it wasn't as steep. Once they reached the ground, they cut their way back to the stream, following the track along the rocky creek.

Sari watched a fish as it leaped out of the water, noticing that everything here seemed brighter and more transparent. The colours were vibrating with brilliant greens, browns and reds. *Maybe this side of the island really is blessed.* The birds twittered high above, and now and then one would swoop across their path showing off a brilliant display of colours. Snakes slithered past with equally impressive colours and even the lizards scampering about seemed to show off, she thought. By the time they had stopped for breakfast, this place had convinced Sari that there was something magical about going on here. She was sure this was paradise and that the Holy Whale had something to do with it. She sat by the stream and watched as the boys took turns in spearing for fish. Chuma proved to be the most proficient, catching four fish within minutes, stabbing them cleanly with his spear made from bone. Netro seemed to take great interest in Chuma's spear, comparing it to his own, which was crafted from wood. She was so excited she forgot her reluctance to share her stories about the Holy Whale with Baruti, who sat watching beside her.

'You know they say he can communicate with you with his mind,' she said.

'Who can?' Baruti asked.

'Why, the Holy Whale, of course.' She ignored his raised eyebrows. 'It's true, he would warn fishermen of great storms coming or volcanos erupting under the ocean, and my grandpapa could talk to him.'

'Why do you think he no longer communicates these things?' Baruti frowned.

She thought about her grandfather taken in the storm and the anger rose in her stomach, but she pushed it down.

'Well, I don't know. We must have angered him,' she whispered.

'You are angry about something?' he said.

She looked deeply into his eyes. She didn't know why she wanted to share her feelings with him. Maybe she knew he would not show her sympathy or try to make her feel better about it. She didn't want to feel better about it.

'My grandfather was taken by a storm, and now the ocean has taken my parents too. Mother Nature has not been kind to us, and yet I used to worship her so...'

'I have seen you pray to the sun goddess.'

'Yes, but no longer to the moon goddess, who controls the water. After what is happening in the forest, I am losing my faith in the sun goddess, too,' she whispered.

'It is our nature to question. Maybe this Holy Whale has the answers,' he said.

Netro joined them, an empty spear in hand. 'That's why we are here, to ask him why he has left us,' he said, placing his spear at his feet.

'And you believe he will communicate with you?' Baruti wanted to know.

'There's always a chance, Baruti, or you wouldn't be here yourself,' he teased.

'I am here on the order of Chief Sakima, to find out who or what is causing these strange happenings, and if I have to talk to a whale to do it, so be it.' He smiled another rare smile, and they all giggled, feeling a little silly.

*S*ari felt she had lightened her load. Excitement had now overcome her nerves, and she was ready to get going once more. She didn't even mind eating raw fish, although secretly she wished they could light a fire and cook it a little.

They packed up and headed into the tree line bordering the stream, their clothes drying as they walked in the brilliant sunshine. The trees could offer little shade from its harsh rays. The rotting leaves underfoot began to dry out, and Raden whistled sweetly ahead of her. Sari noticed that she wasn't getting bitten, which was a pleasant change. Almost abruptly up ahead, Baruti signalled for them all to get down. She waited for the signal to join them. Crouching on all fours, they crept closer to Baruti and Netro at the front of the group. Ahead, just around the bend, there stood some type of fortress close to the bank of the river, a very large, simple, round structure built with mud walls and palm leaves for a roof. Sari estimated it could house at least fifty people.

'What is it?' she whispered to Raden.

'I'm not sure. From the mountain it looked as if their village was by the ocean.'

'Why would they have a structure out here?' she said

'I don't know.' He shook his head.

'Maybe it's a separate tribe?' she offered.

'No, too close to be another tribe; must be the same tribe but living separately for some reason.'

There didn't seem to be any doors to get in from this side, so the group carefully and quietly circled the rounded structure. Around the far side, they found two sets of footholds, which led upward to the top of the wall, but there were no doors or any other way in.

'We'll have to go up and over the wall,' Netro whispered.

Baruti put his finger to his lips and with no further discussion climbed the footholds in the mud wall. Sari looked around her nervously. When Baruti reached the top, he gingerly peered over its rim. Sari held her breath. What he saw must have shaken him. His body tensed, and he stayed up there far longer than she liked. Baruti finally came down and gestured for them to follow him back to the safety of the trees.

They gathered around him as he spoke. 'What I have seen is of great concern, but I am not sure we should stay and get involved. We have a purpose, and I believe we should forget what we have seen here today and continue on. We now know that we will not be greeted with open arms. I am certain the tribe will be hostile.' Baruti interpreted to Chuma.

'Baruti, you must tell us what you have seen. We cannot decide because you say so,' Netro said, squaring his shoulders.

They glared at one another. While Raden and Chuma looked on, Sari got up and slipped away from them. She needed to see for herself what was happening behind those walls. She pushed the sling behind her so Baby could rest on her back and climbed the mud footholds, her heart hammering in her chest. When Sari reached the top, she peered through the gap in the palm fronds. It took her eyes some time to adjust to the darkness, only partially lit by filters of sunlight, which streamed through the palm fronds. She saw them then, sitting there in the mud pit, and she quickly estimated that about twenty to thirty people sat huddled together. Most of them appeared to be sleeping. They were filthy dirty, and the stench overwhelmed her.

The pit had been dug deep into the ground, and the mud

walls had been built up around it. Rats scurried about, negotiating the wet, muddy puddles of the pit.

Netro saw her and called softly, 'Sari, quick, get down.
Someone's coming!'

She scampered down as quickly as she could and
followed Netro back into the safety of the trees. As they
watched, two men arrived carrying a basket between them.
They were short in stature, and Sari guessed that they would
come up to her armpit and she wasn't tall. Their yellow-
skinned bodies were covered in coarse black hair, and they
wore long, black matted hair to their thick waists, where a
simple loincloth made from animal skin hung. Sari noticed
their yellow, flat, blunt teeth as they spoke to each other in
deep grunting voices. Around their short, thick necks they
wore a simple decoration of pearls.

Sari now knew why there were two sets of footholds in
the mud wall, as she watched them scale it with ease,
balancing the basket between them. When they reached the
top, they moved aside some palm fronds and tipped the
contents of their basket over the top of the wall into the pit.
A collective cry came from within the pit walls. The captors
watched, snorting with amusement, and Sari imagined the
people in the hole clambering over one another for food. She
pressed her eyelids together tightly to shut out the image.
She heard the pit people shouting and calling out for help.
She couldn't really understand what they were saying, but
she thought she heard a woman cry out in her own language.

'Please help us. Water.'

Sari knew she must have imagined it, as she doubted
people on this side of the island spoke the same language as
she did.

After taunting their prisoners, the men seemed to lose
interest in the pit and climbed down the wall. They drank
from the creek by planting their entire face directly into the

water. When they had finished, they shook their heads, spraying water all around them, and got to their feet, looking up and down the stream, the smaller one sniffing the wind like a fox.

Sari rubbed her sun carving, thinking of Raden's shadow. She held her breath, sure she was about to be discovered, thankful that Baby slept soundly in her arms.

The smaller man turned on his heel and followed his comrade down the stream.

Raden prodded her in the arm. 'How many people in that pit, Sari?'

'About twenty to thirty.'

'Are they their people?' His eyes were wide.

'I don't know, it's dark in there, and they are filthy. Most of them were sleeping or lying down.' Sari wished she could tell him more.

'Why can't they get out? The wall is not all that high. They could climb on each other, couldn't they?'

'The pit has been dug into the ground. It's deep and muddy, and it's a lot deeper than it looks from the outside.'

She checked the stream to make sure the men were still walking away.

'I wonder how long they have been in there?' he said.

Sari showed him her bravest face. 'I don't know, but while I have breath in my body, I'm getting them out.'

'Hold on,' Netro urged. 'A prisoner is a prisoner for a reason. If those people are from their own tribe, then they have committed some crime against the tribe and will only turn on us if you let them out.'

Sari saw his logic. *Maybe they were dangerous*, she thought. She smiled as Chuma handed her a plate of pineapple and coconut, realising they'd missed lunch by the low position of the sun goddess in the pale blue sky.

'We should take another look and try to find out who

they are,' Raden said, getting to his feet and chewing on a piece of coconut.

'Yes, but we can't let them know we're here. They could turn on us and tell their captors we are here, and that will ruin all our plans to see the Holy Whale,' Netro said, pulling Raden down to his level.

Baruti scoffed. 'You are all foolish; no good can come of this. How will you get them out, and what will you do with them once they are out? If they are captured again, they will speak of us.'

He's back to his usual unpleasant self, Sari thought. She knew he spoke the truth, but something drew her to that pit, and she couldn't leave those people in there to die, although she admitted she felt a little afraid. Those men didn't look friendly, and she didn't like the idea of letting twenty to thirty of their kind loose.

* * *

*a*fter they had eaten, they took turns in peering over the pit to see what each could study about the people inside. Raden saw one man get up and do his business up against the pit wall.

'I am sure that man was much taller than their captors,' he said.

Sari didn't think they were from any one tribe. She believed they were a mix of tribes.

'We need to decide soon what we will do. It will be night-fall soon,' Baruti said, becoming impatient.

'Someone could go into the pit and talk to them,' Sari suggested.

'No one is going in that pit alone. You might not come out alive,' Netro responded, and it reminded her he at least was aware of the danger.

They sat in silence until Baruti spoke. 'If we agree to get them out, how do you intend to do it?'

Netro seemed taken aback. 'We could make a hole in the side of the mud wall and get them out through the hole,' he stammered.

'No, it's too dangerous. You could weaken the mud wall, and the entire thing could collapse on top of them.'

Sari caught Baruti's look of superiority.

'I suggest we make ropes and pull them out over the top,' he said smugly. 'We will help you on one condition.'

'Yes?' Netro said cautiously.

'We do not show ourselves. We throw a rope over, and we allow only one person to climb out. We take the rope away to ensure this. We question him, and then we decide whether to get the rest out. If we decide for whatever reason that we don't want these people out, we dispose of this person,' Baruti said, his tone final.

Sari knew he meant every word. A shudder ran down her spine. 'Why?' she whispered, almost afraid to ask.

'He cannot go back into the pit to tell the others about us; it is too dangerous.'

'You mean you will kill him.'

'Yes.'

They sat in stunned silence, staring at Baruti.

'If we decide we don't want him out, then he must be an evil person,' Netro said, giving Sari's arm a squeeze.

'Agreed then?' Baruti asked.

'Agreed!' Sari's voice sounded reluctant with the others.

Sari just hoped and prayed that the person they took out would be a nice person so they could set them all free.

They worked out that they would need four ropes, so they could throw two down at once and have backups if required. They collected strips of liana vine and were careful to cut the vine where it could not be seen from the track so as not to attract attention. They laid the long strips of vine along the ground and Sari took her three pieces of the vine and knotted them together at one end. She plaited the three vines together to make a single rope and then bound the end once she had finished. Between them, they soon had four long, sturdy ropes. They would need only one for now. Sari hoped they would need all four.

* * *

etro and Baruti climbed the structure once more while the others waited below. They slipped the rope over the wall, lowering it as far as it would go, holding their heads well below the wall so they couldn't be seen. Murmuring came from the pit as the rope smacked the mud walls. It occurred to Sari that they probably wouldn't be able to understand the person they pulled out, anyway. She smiled to herself. *No one had considered that one*, she thought. To confirm her suspicions, a woman called out in a language she had never heard before, and she inadvertently rolled her eyes. Baruti and Netro stayed quiet and held on tightly to the rope draped over the pit wall. Nothing happened. It had gone silent in the pit. No one seemed to want to take the chance, and Sari wasn't surprised.

'What should we do?' Sari heard Netro hiss.

'Just wait,' Baruti urged.

Sari looked at Chuma in the fading light. He shook his head. He obviously didn't believe anyone would climb the rope either. Sari sat down, now bored with it all, and Raden joined her.

'It doesn't look as though anyone wants to be rescued today,' he whispered.

'Would you climb the rope?' she said, studying his face.

'Yes, would you?'

'No, better what you know than what you don't.'

Raden nodded.

Baruti and Netro braced themselves, and Raden tilted his head in their direction.

'What's happening?' she hissed.

'Someone's tugging on the rope,' Netro said, panting with excitement.

They waited.

'Okay, someone is on their way up,' Netro said.

Baruti whispered orders to his men.

Sari and the others moved into the trees out of sight as planned and waited excitedly. They watched as a man's head of wispy grey hair peeked over the pit wall. Sari heard her heart thumping in her chest. Netro and Baruti helped him down over the wall, down the vine, and safely to the ground. Sari watched as Netro and Baruti spoke to him. They seemed to have an actual conversation with the old man.

'What do you think, Raden?' she whispered, prodding him in the arm.

Raden didn't answer her but stared straight ahead, his eyes never leaving the man's face. Without warning, he broke the line of the trees, running towards the man, Baruti and Netro. The man turned to face Raden, and Sari's heart froze in fear. Netro looked at Baruti, grabbing the man's arms as if to protect him somehow. Sari watched in confusion as Raden picked up his pace. The old man cried out as Raden embraced him, lifting him into the air. Sari wasn't sure what she witnessed, but she cried out and ran towards Raden, caught up in an emotion she didn't fully understand.

The old man shouted, 'Raden, Raden?'

Raden cried out, 'Grandpapa you're alive.' They both wept openly.

Sari couldn't breathe because her chest felt so tight. She turned toward the pit, her eyes bulging from her head with the strain of keeping her emotions in check. She stared at the walls as if trying to see through them. Then she ran to the pit and quickly climbed the footholds, her jerky movements waking Baby, who wailed in her arms.

'Sari,' Netro called. 'What are you doing? We need to question...' He trailed off.

She reached the top of the pit and couldn't stop herself screaming into the black hole, 'Mama, Mama? Papa, Papa...?'

Several voices screamed back at her. None was recognisable to Sari. She sobbed loudly now, and people were pulling on the rope. She couldn't hold it, and it flew over the side of the pit wall. Silence fell as the line tumbled down, and then screams of anguish sounded as it fell to the ground.

'Sari, stop it, come down. With all that screaming, they will catch us all.' Netro sounded furious, but she couldn't stop herself.

She felt as though she had lost control of her usually controlled self. 'Mama, Papa, it's Sari,' she cried out again. There was a lot of shushing in the pit. She called again. 'It's Sari.'

There was silence in the pit until a lone woman's voice returned Sari's cry, small but steady. 'Sari?'

She heard her mother's sweet voice and nearly fell into the pit. Baruti climbed up the pit wall and grabbed her ankles and tried to pull her down.

She kicked at him furiously. 'Mama, Mama?' she sobbed. 'It's me, Sari!'

Sari heard the disbelief in her mother's voice. 'Sari? Sari?'

Netro and Raden dragged Sari from the pit wall, sobbing, kicking and lashing out at everyone around her. Baby dug his fingers into her back in protest. Raden embraced her tightly, and she struggled to free herself. Netro placed his hand over her mouth. She sank her teeth into his hand.

'Mama's in the pit, Mama's in the pit,' she screamed at him as Netro removed his hand.

'Sari, calm down, we will get her out now,' Raden pleaded, pulling her away.

She continued to struggle. Baruti scaled the pit wall and gestured for everyone in the pit to quieten down.

Chuma climbed the wall and helped Baruti lower two more ropes. It took some time to work out an order after some initial fighting over who would climb the ropes first.

Raden's grandpapa spoke to Sari in a firm voice. 'Girl, you must be strong for your mother Lena when she comes out of that pit. She has been through a lot.'

His gapped teeth shone in the moonlight and Sari immediately respected her elder and stopped struggling. Netro let her go, taking Chuma's place on the pit wall, but Raden stayed close to her.

'What about my papa?' Sari asked.

He shook his head, and her heart sank. She watched the top of the pit eagerly in the fading light. A woman came out, dark-skinned with wide eyes. She looked fearfully at Netro and Baruti. They helped her over the wall and she joined them. Sari ignored her, too concerned with her mother who came out next. Sari watched as her mother embraced Netro. He helped her to the ground, holding her for a long time. She turned to Sari, with tears streaming down her weary face. Her tears streaked her dirty cheeks, and her long brown hair matted around her ear. *She's still beautiful*, thought Sari, *like a vision of a goddess*. Sari flew into her arms and stayed there until Netro prised them apart to join in.

'My Sari, my Netro,' she said, stroking their hair.

Raden went to help Baruti free the rest of the prisoners.

'My Perak, my baby?' her mother asked.

'He is safe,' Netro assured. 'And Papa?'

She shook her head. 'We were separated, so I don't know.

Let us sit somewhere and talk. I can see that you have grown into a fine young man while I have been away, Netro, your papa would be proud.' She looked away sadly.

'Thank you, Mama,' he said.

They moved away from the others and spoke among themselves while they watched prisoner after prisoner come over the pit wall. The black of night enveloped them as the last person came out. Time had stood still for Sari while her mother had held her in her arms. She looked around at the people from all parts of the island. She recognised a few faces from her own village, and she saw Baruti and Chuma embracing a few of their own tribe members. Some were from the north and some from the south of the island.

They all took a long drink from the creek, and Sari led her mother over to join them. Some washed their faces; some stared up at the moon goddess and smiled. *They were free, but what now?* Sari assumed they would rest and get going again in the morning. She watched her mother wash her face.

'I see you have a new friend, my Sari, reminds me of your papa's shadow,' her mother said, stroking Baby's cheek.

'Yes, me too, we have so much to tell you, Mama.'

'And I you, my Sari, I wished many times my shadow parrot was still with me and could somehow fly me away from this place, but I wasn't just talking about the monkey,' she said, looking towards Raden who was in deep conversation with his grandpapa.

Sari blushed. 'Oh, Mama.'

They giggled as they watched the debating going on within the large group.

'I'll find out what's going on,' Sari said, moving a few feet from her mother to where Raden now stood alone.

'We are going again soon,' Raden said.

'Why can't we rest here tonight and work it out tomorrow?' she asked.

117

'The men will come back at first light to check on the pit.' Raden sighed.

'What's the matter?' Sari noticed that Raden's earlier happiness seemed to have faded.

'It's my grandmama. She didn't make it; she died in that pit,' he spat.

'Oh, Raden, I'm so sorry.'

She wanted to comfort him but wasn't sure how.

She nodded her head in his direction. 'Who is that talking to your grandpapa?' '

'It's my aunt and uncle.'

'That's wonderful news, so you have found them all. I mean, I'm sorry about your grandmama.'

'What does your mama know about your papa?' he asked, changing the subject for her.

'Mama said they were separated. She doesn't know what happened to him, but it is known in the pit they are using strong men in the village as workers, so she hopes he could be there.'

Raden pushed back one of Sari's stray locks of hair from her eyes. 'There is always hope, Sari.'

* * *

They stood together silently and watched as some of the prisoners melted into the trees. The prisoners said their farewells and thanks and they were gone. Sari understood that they wanted to get as far away as possible from this place. They just wanted to get home to their families. She knew how they felt.

Raden took her arm and led her back to her mother.'I guess we should work out what we are doing,' he said.

They found Lena chatting quietly with another woman from the pit.

'Mama, I'm just going to talk to Netro,' she said, reluctant to leave her.

Lena cupped Raden's cheek. 'I'm pleased to see you, Raden. Your grandpapa was a great comfort to me, as I know you have been a great comfort to my Sari. Thank you.'

Sari noticed that he reddened under her touch.

'I'm very pleased to see you also,' he mumbled.

'Go now, I'll be fine, and I'll wash my hair.' Her mother smiled.

Sari could hardly believe that her mother was here in front of her.

'I will have to leave her again, won't I?' Sari sighed as they walked away.

Raden didn't answer her. They approached Netro, who was learning quickly every manner of greeting, farewells, and thank-you's in every language.

'Have a safe journey,' Netro called, turning to them.

'So you are a hero. What's next?' she teased.

'Let's talk to Baruti,' he said thoughtfully.

Baruti was already approaching, and Sari knew he would have a plan of action figured out. I *guess that's what leaders are for*; she thought.

'Most are happy to find their own way home to their tribes,' Baruti began. 'We have rescued three members of our own tribe and they will return to Chief Sakima. They can take your mother and Raden's relatives to our tribe, and they can stay on as Chief Sakima's guests and wait for your return or continue on home if they wish.'

Sari watched her mother by the stream, her heart squeezing in her chest. Sari knew this was the safest option for her mother and relented.

'You want to go with her, Sari?' Netro asked.

She shook her head. 'No, I need to help to find Papa.'

'You want me to tell her?' Netro offered.

'No, I'll tell her. Just come with me.' She sighed, offering him a weak smile.

They ambled over to join Lena.

'Mama,' they said together.

She turned, and her deep green eyes looked into Sari's. Sari sat down beside her, placing her head on her shoulder.

'We need to continue on our journey. The map shows that it's only another day's walk away. Netro needs to help our tribe, and I need to find Papa.'

'And me?' she breathed.

'They want you to return with the others to Chief Sakima's tribe and wait for us there or go on home if you wish.'

'I have no home without my family,' she said sadly.

Sari knew she thought of her husband.

'Perak waits for you with Chief Sakima.'

Lena's eyes lifted. 'Perak?'

'Yes, he came with us into the forest, but things became too dangerous.'

'You left him alone in a strange village?' she gasped.

Sari, feeling scolded, looked into her hands in shame.

Netro came to her defence. 'I promise you, Mama, he was safer with them than with us.'

Lena looked over to Baruti and his men with suspicion clear in her eyes, and after a moment she spoke. 'You have each other. Perak needs me and I am too weak, so I will go, but before you go, I want to know all about your journey so far.'

Sari breathed a sigh of relief and looked up, searching her mother's face for a sign of forgiveness.

'You first, Mama. What happened to you and Papa on the beach when the wave came? How did you get here?'

Her mother frowned. 'It seems like the strangest dream now and I'm not sure you would believe me, my Sari if I told you. Still, I will tell you what I remember.' She sighed, taking

Sari and Netro's hands into hers. 'The wave came, and it swept us under, your father never letting go of my hand.' She paused. 'We tumbled together in the waves, and then we were dry, lying on the back of an enormous whale as it coasted along. I remember little more. We woke up on a beach, your papa still holding my hand in his. These horrible little men waved spears in our faces, and they forced us apart. I have not seen your papa since.' A tear welled in her eye.

'It will be all right now, Mama,' Netro said.

'Tell me about your adventure. You will have some explaining to do, my Netro, when the elders next see you, but don't worry too much, I hear they have some explaining of their own,' she said.

Sari and Netro exchanged a quick look. Sari took as much food as she could spare from their supplies and shared it with her mother. They sat with her and ate, regaling her in all their adventures, good and bad. Sari saw the fear in her mother's eyes as they told her of the giant butterflies and the strange happenings that they had encountered along the way, but there were no tears when they finally left her.

'Netro, look after your sister, and you tell that whale we are decent people who deserve better.'

'I will, Mama.'

She hugged him tightly and kissed him on the forehead. He held back his tears.

'Sari, you bring all our men home to me.'

Sari felt the lump forming in her throat. 'I'll try, Mama.'

'I know you will.'

She held Sari for a long time, and she felt her mother's body shake with the force of trying to control her emotions. They walked slowly away from her mother's group into the forest and walked with their own group downstream.

8

WHALE CRY

*T*he moon goddess shone her full face down upon them as they walked beside the water's edge. Its beams danced across the stream, the water washing downward toward their destination. Sari had a spring in her step. Seeing her mother had renewed her energy. She still had so many unanswered questions, but she now believed her papa to be alive.

Chuma and Raden walked further back and she let them catch up to her. 'Did your grandpapa know anything about the Holy Whale? Has he seen it, Raden?'

'No, nothing; there were rumours, but he didn't see it. They were captured in the woods, so he has never been to the main village, ' he sighed.

'What's wrong?' she said.

He trailed a stick behind him in the dirt. 'My grandpapa says that when the elders banished them, a group of boys followed them and tried to kill them,' he hesitated, ' and he believes they were from our tribe. He has no proof, but he believes the elders sent them.'

Sari's eyes widened. 'Why, for speaking out against them?'

'They questioned the elders about their wealth, and they didn't like it.'

'That can't be the only reason.'

'No, he also believes they came close to finding out what happened to the Holy Whale when they found a pearl like the one Netro found, and that was the real reason why the elders wanted to be rid of them.'

'Did the pearl have a message?'

'They didn't get that far, they were seen with it, and the elders took it.'

'How did they get away from the bandits?'

'He said he did what he had to do to protect his family and escape.'

'I understand.' Sari sighed.

'Only to be captured again by another tribe.' Raden scowled, throwing his stick into the trees.

'Netro, are you hearing this? Did any of the prisoners say anything about a pearl, about bandits or whales?' she said, pulling on the back of his tunic.

Netro pulled his body away sharply.'No.'

'I must know, do you believe the Holy whale is still there?'

'I still hope, but I'm not sure now. How could all those people know nothing? Some say they have been to the village, but many seasons ago,' he said, kicking the ground in frustration.

'What do they say about the village and its people?' she asked.

'They say the village is like paradise with all the foods and supplies you ever dreamed of and more. You can trade food for weapons or jewellery or gems, anything in your wildest dreams.'

He didn't sound very excited to Sari.

'Be quiet. We are nearing the outskirts of the village,'

Baruti barked over his shoulder. 'Unless you want to spend the rest of your days in a pit, be quiet.'

Sari felt duly scolded and hung her head as she followed Baruti with the group into the forest, where they stumbled and crunched leaves underfoot in the darkness.

Sari heard a rustling in the trees above her head. Looking up, she saw a long black tail disappear. Baby squirmed in her sling.

'She wants to get out; let her ride on your shoulders for a while,' said Raden.

Baby sat happily on Sari's left shoulder, pulling leaves from the trees as they walked. She let out a few whooping noises in her excitement, her nostrils flaring.

'He smells something,' said Netro.

'She,' Sari corrected.

It was quiet, and Sari had seen no one, not even a village of any kind, but she could smell the ocean. She drew its salty smell entirely into her lungs as they neared the edge of the forest. Baruti signalled for them to crouch down. Holding his finger to his lips, he silenced them.

It pleased Sari that they would arrive under the cover of darkness. As she crouched down, Baby jumped from her shoulders and scarpered off through the bushes.

'Baby,' she called quietly.

Baby ignored her, running for the beach. Sari ran, following Baby.

The group called after her, 'Sari, wait.'

She lunged forward, grabbing Baby by the tail. Toppling forward, Sari braced herself for the fall, but landed so softly that she almost bounced, and then she began to sink. The moon shone down on the pool of blackness as she looked around, grappling for something to hold on to. Baby ran up her arm. The group caught up to her as Baby perched on her head, fingering her nose.

'What is this?' she screamed as it sucked her legs from beneath her.

'Black quicksand,' Raden answered. 'You must keep still.'

She wriggled, trying to free herself.

'Sari listen to me. You must keep still. You will go down quicker if you move,' Raden said.

'Just get me out of here,' she cried.

Baruti barked orders to Chuma, and he ran off with Netro to find a branch to pull her out. Raden turned to leave as Sari sank lower, up to her chest.

'Raden, please don't leave me here.'

'I'm going to find something to get you out.'

'No, please... just stay and talk to me.'

'Okay, Sari, I won't leave you,' he said gently.

Baby sat quietly on her head hiccupping. Netro came back with a large branch. They held it out to Sari, and she gripped it tightly, her movement causing her to sink lower into the black abyss.

'Pull,' ordered Raden.

They pulled, but Sari did not move. Baruti and Chuma gripped the branch.

'One, Two, Three, pull...'

The four men fell backwards. Sari sank up to her neck. They got up, grappling for the branch, which threatened to sink into the black sandy bog.

'Position your feet so they won't slide,' instructed Raden. They offered the branch again, and Sari gripped it tightly with both hands.

'Again, pull,' they chorused.

The branch slipped through Sari's hands, and they fell backwards on top of one another. Tears slid down Sari's sand-covered cheeks as she struggled to keep her arms above the sand line.

'Again.'

They repositioned themselves and held out the branch to Sari. She gripped the branch, squeezing her eyes shut as they pulled.

The branch slipped from her hands and they fell backwards again.

Netro pulled his hair in frustration. 'Why is it not working?'

Raden shook his head. 'The angle is all wrong.'

Netro shouted at his friend in desperation. 'Do something.'

'Let me think.'

'Baruti, tell me what to do,' Netro pleaded.

'I'm sorry, Netro, we have no knowledge of these things deep in the forest.'

Netro beat his head with his hands in frustration. Chuma crouched at the bog's edge, staring intently at Sari. Raden looked around frantically. He saw some vines hanging above her head, but she was too low down to reach them, and he was too far away. Sari sobbed.

'It's okay Sari, I will get you out, I promise. Don't cry, please keep still,' Raden pleaded.

'I'm going to die, aren't I?' she gasped.

'Listen to me. I will not let you die; my life is your life. You are my life.'

Their eyes locked, and he said, 'That's right, just look at me, Sari. I will get you out.'

Raden grimaced as she sank lower. The black sand rose to her lips, but she managed to keep her arms free.

'What are you going to do?' Netro asked.

'Shush. I don't know yet. Let me think,' he whispered, staring at Sari. Suddenly he sprang into action. 'Baby, come to me,' he said, holding his arms out to the monkey.

'Yes, save Baby,' Sari gulped.

The monkey didn't respond.

'Tell her to come to me Sari, hurry.'

'Go away Baby, go,' she chided.

Baby still sat, fingering her nose.

'You must shout at her, scare her,' Raden said.

'Shoo. Go away, you horrible monkey. Go!' She looked up at the moon goddess. 'Forgive me,' she whispered.

Baby, never having heard her speak harshly before, jumped from her head into Raden's outstretched arms. He caught Baby and held her high above his head, shaking her from side to side. Baby squealed in protest.

'What are you doing?' muttered Netro.

'Just wait.'

'Stop it, please,' Sari cried.

'Just trust me, Sari, keep still and close your mouth.'

He continued to shake the monkey until her squeals became howls. They heard a rustling in the trees above Sari's head. A black monkey with silver-tipped fur, like the ones they had seen in the forest, clung to a long vine and swung across the black sand toward Baby. The adult monkey tipped upside down as it approached, wrapping its tail around the vine, reaching out to Baby with both hands while hanging by its tail. Baby instinctively held up its arms and clasped hands with the adult monkey. Baby swung onto the adult's back as it righted itself. Before they could swing away, Raden caught the vine, pulling hard. The adult monkey scurried up the vine with Baby on its back and leapt towards the safety of the trees. Raden pulled on the vine, testing his weight briefly, and then, wrapping his legs around the vine, he swung out to Sari as the black sand covered her mouth. He swung over her head and back, waiting for the vine to slow from a full swing to a hover. He hung directly above her, spinning slowly. When the vine stopped, Sari reached out to him. Raden caught her hand in his. He gripped her tightly with his free hand reaching down towards her, while her other hand wrapped around the bottom of the vine and she tried to help pull herself up. Raden's sweat dripped onto her face. His biceps bulged with the effort of dragging her weight upwards.

Netro called out encouragement. 'Yes, the angle is much better. Come on Raden, you can do this.'

The sand gave a little. She pulled with one hand and he pulled with his free hand while holding on tightly to the vine with his other one. The bog began to release her, and they could both feel it.

He exhaled loudly. 'You see.'

The bog made a sucking sound as her chest came free, but his other hand slipped down the vine with the weight of her.

'Raden, can you hold her?' Baruti called.

Sari looked at his hand on the vine, which had started to bleed.

'Oh Raden,' she cried.

'Keep looking at me Sari,' he groaned.

She looked deeply into his eyes.

'I will not let you go,' he said through gritted teeth and let out a roar of determination, yanking her with all his might.

Her legs came free, and she kicked the last of the black sand from her legs in defiance as he pulled her up and into his arms, where she clung to his chest, which rose and fell in time with his heavy breathing. The vine spun them around slowly, and Sari felt Raden's hold tighten on her more as he swung the vine. They moved slowly at first, but the vine soon swung freely.

'I will tell you when to let go,' he instructed.

They swung over Netro's head.

'Now.'

She clung to him, missing her chance as they swung back over the quicksand.

'I can't, I'm afraid,' she whimpered.

'Sari, you have never been afraid in your life, and you can't start now.'

'I can't...'

'Okay Sari, it's all right. Netro, you must grab Sari as we come by.'

Netro stood ready to catch her, pulling her from Raden as they passed. Raden swung back over the bog one more time before returning to them and dropping a few feet away.

The three huddled together for a long time, holding each other.

'Thank you,' Sari murmured.

'Thank you, Raden, you saved her life,' said Netro, the words catching in his throat.

Baruti and Chuma joined them, patting Raden on the shoulders.

Sari's legs gave way under her and Raden scooped her into his arms.

'Let me, you must be tired,' said Netro.

Raden shook his head.

'Where's Baby?' she murmured.

Chuma pointed into a tree above them. Baby sat on the adult monkey's back, staring at her.

'Goodbye Baby,' she whispered, passing out in Raden's arms.

* * *

They arrived under cover of darkness as planned, the sun yet to rise by the time they reached the long stretch of beach which led down to the shoreline. They stayed within the thin cover of the trees and looked up and down the beach. Sari thought they must be lost. She couldn't see anything but sand. To her right, the beach ended with a wall of rocks, and to her left the beach stretched endlessly. She saw no end.

Netro consulted the map with Baruti looking over his shoulder.

'What does the map say?' she asked.

'The map ends here,' he said, pointing to the ground. 'We are where we are meant to be.'

He sounded a little puzzled. Sari felt flat. She looked at the faces of her companions and knew they were feeling the same way. She stared back at the ocean but couldn't see anything but blackness lapping against the shore.

'Well, do we go towards the rocks or to the never-ending beach?' she said, pulling on her brother's sleeve.

'Let's see what's over those rocks; the village must be there,' Netro reasoned, looking to Baruti for support. Baruti merely nodded in approval.

It wasn't a long walk to the rocks, but they stayed close to the tree line, so as not to be seen, and Raden stayed close to Sari. She was more aware of him than she had ever been. When they reached the rocks, they had a choice of either climbing up and over them or following them back around into the forest. They had no access via the ocean, as it was too dangerous.

'It will be better to see from above,' Baruti grunted with his usual abruptness, snapping his fingers to Chuma.

Chuma jumped to attention and climbed the wall of rocks, taking the lead. Sari looked to Netro for direction, but he shrugged and followed Chuma up the wall of black rocks. Sari followed, gingerly placing her foot on the first wet and slippery black rock. Raden helped Sari from behind by gently nudging her forward. Something had changed between them. Her heart hammered in her chest at his closeness, and she could feel his body heat behind her, urging her upwards. Netro offered his hand to her from in front as they climbed toward the sound of crashing waves. The cold wind whipped through Sari's tunic, making her legs shake. She lost her footing and held her breath in anticipation of the fall, but Raden stopped her from behind with his broad frame. She leaned against him for a second longer than necessary, her skin tingling with excitement.

Netro turned and pulled her up towards the top of the rocky ledge. They joined the others, crouching down almost lying flat on the icy rocks. A gust of wind and sea spray slapped Sari in the face as she peered over the cliff. They gasped as they took in the scene before them. The noise of crashing waves deafened them now. Sari's lips quivered. There wasn't a village as she had expected, but another bay and a huge white whale languished in its waters. It was so large it took up nearly the whole bay from the rocks where they watched to the rocks on the other side of the bay. From Sari's vantage point, the whale looked to be pure white from its flippers to its fluke. *This must be the Holy Whale.* Its massive white head faced the shoreline, and its tail stretched back out toward the ocean. The whale's flippers were nearly as long as its body, and it blew vapour from its blowhole, shooting the fine mist mixed with mucus into the air above. The smooth body of brilliant white thrashed from side to side beneath the water, glowing in the moonlight. It stopped thrashing as if it was resting, and the crashing waves subsided. Sari saw one of its huge round black eyes on the side of its head swivel in her direction, and she had an overwhelming feeling that the Holy Whale looked directly at her.

After a few minutes' rest, the whale went slightly under the water and thrashed its tail on the surface as if in protest. Sari realised the whale must be tied up; somehow, its movement seemed restricted. She couldn't see what held the whale under the water and she strained her eyes in the darkness. She looked up and down the bay, her eyes settling on the empty beach. No one seemed to watch the whale in its struggle for freedom. Sari looked over at Netro's grief-stricken face.

'How can they hold him? No ropes could hold a whale of its size,' he murmured to Baruti.

'We must find out,' Baruti said, the whites of his eyes nodding with his head.

Netro said, 'Baruti and I will look into it further. We need to get to the rocks on the other side and find the villagers. Stay here with the others and keep watch. It will be quicker this way.'

Before she could protest, Netro and Baruti clambered over the rocks. Chuma followed them until Baruti snapped at him in his own tongue.

She watched them descend towards the beach, keeping an eye on the tree line for any activity. The Holy Whale bobbed quietly now, and Sari revelled in his magnificence.

She had so many questions swimming around in her head. *Why would these people capture and keep the whale? Surely this would not bring them good fortune.*

* * *

*T*he sun goddess threatened to make her appearance, and Netro and Baruti had not returned. A parade of men marched out through the forest and onto the beach. Watching from above, Sari flattened her body on the cold rocks along with the others. The Holy Whale must have sensed their presence and began thrashing around after having been quiet for so long. Sari saw that the men were prisoners and her heart leapt, thinking of her papa. Several captors carrying clubs flanked the prisoners. They were the same in stature and appearance as those who had fed the prisoners in the pit. She recognised their short-hairy bodies and the same unkempt long black hair. The prisoners carried large black rocks between them in pairs. Sari studied each of the prisoners' faces carefully for her papa. They struggled under the weight of the boulders, one pair dropping their heavy load into the sand. Their captors, small, but vicious, set upon them with clubs. The beating subsided, and the men got slowly to their feet, lifting the rock between them. The line of men continued on toward the rock wall. Once there, they were instructed where to place their rock along the wall. None of them resembled her papa. Sari's attention drew back to the forest as another line of men emerged. This time marching in single file and jostling along, encouraged by their captors who once again wielded clubs almost half their size. They marched toward the water and waded in, diving quickly under the waves and trying to avoid the whale's flippers. The great whale continued to thrash about, creating waves, which crashed against the rocks and slammed into the beach.

Sari had had no time to study the men and wondered if her papa had been among them. One man with very pale skin misjudged his dive and as he entered the water one of the whale's flippers crashed down on top of him. Sari winced. The man rolled over in the water, and the next wave carried him toward the beach, landing him face first upon the sand. He lay motionless. His two captors dragged him by his feet, dragging his face in the sand as they pulled him up the beach and left him there.

Sari squinted to see in the emerging light. 'What are the divers doing? Have they come to feed him?'

'It looks as if they are tightening the restraints.' Raden rubbed his eyes. 'I can't see what they hold in their hands, but it's something small.'

Sari felt her panic rising and she pulled her tunic closer to her slight frame. 'The sun is almost up. What should we do? I thought they would be back by now.'

To her surprise, the men were coming out of the water. They walked back up the beach in pairs, shaking the water from their bodies as they walked. Two of them stopped and crouched over their fallen comrade, picked him up and carried him away into the forest.

'That was quick. What do we do now?' Sari asked.

Sari didn't know what to make of it all; why did no one feed the whale? She knew whales ate a lot. Her grandpapa had told her so.

'What holds him?' Raden said, shaking his head. 'With all that thrashing about you would think he could free himself.'

'Let's wait here for Netro for as long as we can. We seem safe here.'

The three companions waited on the rocks all day waiting for Netro and Barutis' return. Sari forced herself to act sensibly around Raden by making polite conversation, and at times she would catch his eyes on her, and he would quickly look away. This both pleased and frightened her. Chuma had made several trips down the other side of the rocks to the waterline to collect shellfish for them to eat. He was an essential part of their group, and she wished she could explain this to him. They watched the activities on the beach. The same routine seemed to repeat several times throughout the day. Men brought rocks and risked their lives entering the water. The second shift of men caught Sari's attention. One man walked in a way familiar to her. He was too thin to be her papa, his skin was darker, and his hair was too long, but something about him drew her eyes to him every time he did his rounds. He entered the water grace-fully, and Sari held her breath and waited for him to resur-face. She felt relieved each time he made it back to the shore. The more she watched him, the more she imagined it was him. Sari tried to press her hopes down, but they would surface again each time she saw him.

Raden wouldn't say for sure if it was him or not. 'It could be him, but we are too far away to tell. At nightfall we will go and find this prisoner camp and see for ourselves.'

He tried to reassure her by patting her arm.

She sighed with relief. She knew Raden would help her, but who would help the Holy Whale?

They ate more of their supplies and waited as nightfall came. Raden did his best to interpret to Chuma their plan to find the prison camp. Chuma pointed silently to the foot of the rocks where two figures climbed. Netro panted heavily from the climb. Sari explained what they had seen that day and their desire to see the camp. The look on Netro's face stopped Sari midway through her storytelling.

'What's wrong?'

He sighed, rubbing his eyes, and spoke softly against the roar of the waves behind him. The wind caught his words. 'On the other side of these rocks is another bay like this one.' He put his head in his hands. 'It holds a mother whale and her baby.'

'No,' Sari gasped, looking once more towards the Holy Whale in the fading light.

She felt a little relieved; it wasn't bad news about her papa, but she felt sad for Netro and the whales.

'We watched the same thing in the next bay, with the carrying of rocks and the men going in the water. On the other side of that bay is the village. There are many people, and it's busy, but there is also something you never want to see.'

His lip trembled, and Sari felt sure there was news of her papa.

'What?'

He lowered his voice further. 'Men come in boats. They

135

bring treasures, the likes of which we have never seen, with bright colours, and weaves softer than you can imagine. People wear them, these bright colours, and there are spices, the smell, the food I cannot describe.'

'Why do they bring these things?' she asked

A tear slid down his cheek. 'In exchange for the whales.'

'There are more whales?'

The drone of Baruti's voice slightly distracted her as he interpreted to Chuma.

'They kill the whales, Sari,' he sobbed.

Raden looked away.

'But why?' She shook her head, disturbed by her brother's tears. She had never seen him cry; not even when their parents had gone missing.

'I don't know. I think they must eat the whale meat and use it for trade,' he said, his face contorted.

'Where do they do this? I must see it for myself.'

'I told you... on the other side of the village, and you must not go there. The ocean runs red with their blood.' Fresh tears slid down his face. 'I never want to go there again; the smell is like rotten meat and fish.'

She looked at Baruti, his eyes drawn in anger as he explained to Chuma.

Sari put her arm around Netro's shoulders.

'Of course I will not go there. We will never go there again. I promise.'

Sari waited for Netro to calm himself. 'So, what do we do now? This all seems beyond our help,' she said, looking to Raden who had turned away from them.

'Raden?'

'Let us see if we can find your papa first,' he said. 'Perhaps we can free some more prisoners and then maybe we should go home and leave this place forever.'

'We cannot leave the whales.' Netro spat the words through his misery.

Sari frowned, Netro's tears forgotten. 'Oh, and what should we do? Take on the whole tribe and set the whales free and risk our own lives?' she said, getting up and shaking her head in amazement.

'Yes,' Netro shouted. 'You forget the strange happenings on the island and what waits for us at home. Our village will soon be wiped out if we don't do something soon.'

'And what does any of this have to do with our village?' Sari opened her arms wide.

Netro jumped to his feet, glaring at her, inches from her face. 'More than you know. I think the slaughter of the whales is causing some imbalance in nature; it's all connected.'

Raden pushed a space between them. 'Look, let's just find your papa and decide after that. This is getting us nowhere.' Raden sighed and addressed Baruti. 'Is that okay with you, Baruti?'

Baruti raised his eyebrows. He seemed to be surprised that Raden had addressed him.

'Yes, he nodded, I hope these prisoners will have the answers we seek. They are witness to all that goes on here.'

Sari thought she had heard something. 'Shush.'

They all stayed perfectly still. Peering over the rock wall, Sari saw a lone figure climbing toward them.

'It's not one of them,' Netro whispered, the argument forgotten.

'How do you know?' Sari whispered back.

'Too tall.'

* * *

*T*he figure climbed steadily.

'What shall we do? There is nowhere to hide,' Sari said, looking around for an escape.

Instead, she followed Baruti's lead and lay as flat as she could amongst the rocks, their sharp edges digging into her side. The others followed in silence. Sari listened to her own silent breathing as the waves lapped, and the Holy Whale bobbed quietly below.

Sari took another look; the figure came closer and she watched in horror as Baruti aimed his bow and arrow.

'No,' she protested.

Baruti waved her away, putting his finger to his lips. He raised his aim. The figure stopped as if sensing danger and spoke into the wind. 'I must speak with the child, Sari,' the man said.

No one moved. Baruti signalled wildly for Sari to stay hidden. The man spoke in a tongue familiar to Sari and Netro, a language that had been taught to them by their grandpapa, a language like their own, but more clipped and gruffer,

'I have a message for ye,' the man called.

Sari thought of her papa. She opened her mouth to speak, but Netro put his hand over her mouth gently.

Netro replied for her. 'Who inquires after my sister Sari?'

'The name's Fisk, ye must be Netro.'

Sari and Netro eyed one another in the fading light.

'I'm a fisherman from over the sea. I knew ye grandpapa.'

'How did you know we were here?' Netro asked suspiciously. 'And why do you want to speak with Sari?'

'Am I to talk to rocks and oncoming darkness all night, or will ye show yerselves?'

Sari stood up abruptly, moving toward the man's voice. The others held back and watched while Netro hissed at her but got to his feet and followed. The man sat down on a rock as they approached, gesturing for them to join him. He held out his hand in greeting and Sari gave the old man's weathered hand a limp shake. She studied his pale skin, brilliant blue eyes, and silky white hair. She decided she felt comforted by his presence.

'Do you have a message for me from my papa?'

He looked slightly confused. 'I have no news of ye papa. Are ye here to find him?'

He chewed on the end of a twig, waiting for her to speak.

'Yes, we lost him in the great wave. We have found my mama, and we hoped he might be here.' She sighed, disappointed once more.

'They might hold him in the prison,' he offered kindly, looking toward the beach. 'Silent isn't he?' he added.

They followed his gaze toward the whale. Fisk's eyes clouded over.

'I've been told that ye have come to help me free him.'

Netro greeted him with suspicion in his voice. 'Who told you this?'

'He did.' Fisk nodded his head towards the ocean.

They stared at Fisk and then back at the whale.

Netro's excitement bubbled to the surface. 'So, it's true he can communicate with us.'

Fisk winked. 'Only with a select few.'

Netro waved for the others to join them and relayed what had been said.

Baruti looked suspiciously at the old man, arching his eyebrows. 'And the message for Sari?'

Fisk stared into her eyes. 'The great white whale wants ye to know that we are all connected.'

'What is that supposed to mean?' Netro asked accusingly.

They all turned to Sari. Looking down at her feet, she let the guilt seep into her bones. She knew that she had wanted to find her papa and leave this place. She knew she would have encouraged them all to go. She also knew she would have left the whales in their misery and justified it to herself and the others. *Mother Nature had let them down. What did she owe Mother Nature? Nothing! Why should she help her?* That's what she had thought. She felt guilty now, and weak and ashamed. Only she understood what the Holy Whale had meant.

She had lost her faith, and because of this she was prepared to let nature suffer.

The old man continued to chew steadily. 'The message is for the girl alone, so let her sit with it.'

The last thing Sari wanted to do was sit with it. She pulled the stick from Fisk's mouth and threw it aside.

'Tell us your story. How did you get here? What do we do now?' she demanded.

Netro jumped in. 'Yes, tell us what you know. We have travelled from afar to help.'

Fisk scratched his head. Taking another stick from his pocket, he placed it between his teeth while narrowing his eyes as if to say, *don't do that again.*

'We don't have much time. I'll explain quickly. I came here on me boat from over the seas from the north. I met with their chief, Chief Abog, a delightful fellow. He spoke with me cause he hoped I wanted to trade for the whale meat. I told him what I knew about the whale cries.'

Netro sat forward with his head in his hands, listening attentively. 'What about the whale's cries?'

'The great whale is sending out distress signals under the water, and it is attracting many other whales to the area. This pleases them as the whales are easy prey, but what they don't understand is that the whale's distress signals are causing disturbances to the ocean floor. Many islands have been destroyed, and many lives lost,' he spat.

'We have had many great waves that have damaged our village too. We thought they were tidal waves,' Netro said.

'Not tidal waves; they're waves created by the white whale cries and the other whales. The damage is not as bad here as on the surrounding islands. Ye be only feeling the aftershock of the waves. The whale signals bounce off the surrounding islands, making the islands quake and crumble into the ocean,' he said, and he spat into the rocks.

Sari gasped, covering her mouth. 'What did their chief say, this Abog?'

'He's an ignorant man. They seized me boat and me men and are holding me men in that prison down there. I was lucky to escape before they could capture me.'

'You have seen the prison?' Netro asked.

'Indeed, it's nothing to worry about.'

Raden interpreted to Baruti, who struggled with some of Fisk's words.

'When were your men captured?' Baruti joined the conversation.

Old man Fisk looked Baruti over with his piercing blue eyes before answering. 'A short time ago, and we must free them tonight before they post more men around the prison.'

Sari clenched her bow and arrow. 'And then?'

'We free the white whale and his family, and then the other whales will follow the great white whale out of here, never to return.'

Netro stood ready. 'When do we go?'

'Now,' Fisk got to his feet. 'I've studied the prison and the guards, so follow me.'

They quickly got to their feet, gathered their belongings and followed Fisk down the rock face.

9

DEADLY BEAUTY

*S*ari couldn't believe what they were doing. She felt
she was being dragged into something that didn't
concern her. She thought again of the Holy Whale's message;
we are all connected. All she cared about was her family and
had there not been a slim chance that her papa was impris-
oned behind those walls she would have refused to go. Guilt
dragged at her insides, but she was honest with herself.

They clambered down the rocks toward the beach. The
Holy Whale had gone silent, and Sari worried whether he
might be sick. The men had come again before dark to check
on his restraints just after they had met Fisk.

Fisk led them on a short walk back into the forest and
along a narrow track which led to the prison. They walked
silently; the sand hiding their footfalls. When they reached
the prison, they crouched together watching the hairy men
posted around the prison's mud walls. This wasn't a pit like
the other prison. It had a large door made of palm leaves, but
otherwise, the walls were crafted from the same brown mud,
mixed with sand in the shape of a dome. Sari pushed the
memory of the quicksand from her mind. They crept around

the prison through the forest, keeping their distance. Sari realised that the captors did not expect any opposition. The few guards that were posted around the prison slouched against the mud walls with their clubs discarded at their feet. Only the two men posted on the front entrance looked alert.

'Wait here, Netro, and I will scout the back wall of the prison,' Fisk instructed.

Fisk nodded to Sari as he posted the others around the prison, watching the guards from the thick of the trees.

Sari watched as Fisk took one guard from behind and knocked him unconscious, dragging him into the trees and dropping him at Sari's feet. Netro clobbered the other guard and pulled him into the trees and placed him at Raden's feet. She bit her lip as Netro and Fisk went back to the wall and cut a tiny hole in the back of the prison's mud wall. Fisk whispered through the wall. Sari couldn't hear what was being said, but she wished they would hurry. Terrified of being discovered, she stared down at the man at her feet, the scent of him filling her nostrils. Sari didn't like the way he smelled, like dead fish. *Probably dead whale*, she thought and gave him a poke with her bow. His hairy chest wheezed up and down, undisturbed.

Finally, Netro came back. 'Fisk talked to his men, and they counted forty-two men and no women inside. They say if we are to free the whales we must do it before they return to the beach to drug them.'

'Drug them?' Sari couldn't believe her ears.

'Yes, this is how they can keep the Great White Whale tied.'

'Drug him with what?' she muttered.

She checked on the man at her feet as he groaned.

'There is a plant in the forest, but we will know more soon. Fisk's men don't know everything, so he's talking to some of the other prisoners,' he whispered.

He then slunk back over to Fisk, who spoke now more loudly than Sari would have liked through the hole. Fisk grew silent for some time, listening to what was being said on the other side while they waited anxiously, Sari chewing her nails and then starting in on her hair. Fisk was talking again and suddenly broke off his conversation through the mud wall.

Sari whispered what she had seen and what Netro had told her to Raden, and he passed it on down the line.

Fisk finally got to his feet, and they gathered together once more as a group. The look on his face worried Sari.

'Setting the men and the whales free is not our problem.' Fisk sighed.

'What now?' Sari moaned.

'There's a plant not far from here. They call it *yeva*. Ye could call it magical, or ye could call it deadly. It is both. The sap is a kind of magical poison. They tell me that an animal that eats the sap of this tree will become the opposite of what it is, so a strong whale becomes weak, or sometimes it can just die from the poison.' He chewed on a fresh stick and spat into the dirt. 'This is also why they don't have te feed the whale.'

'What do you mean?' Sari asked.

'They can drug the whale and keep it strong at the same time,' Fisk said.

'So, they don't have to feed it?' Netro groaned.

'And, the Holy Whale could have been here for a long time,' Sari stammered.

Netro shook his head sadly. 'That's why we haven't seen any whales for a long time.'

'The butterflies must have come in contact with the sap of this yeva tree,' Sari gasped, turning to Raden.

'You could be right. There is no other explanation for giant butterflies that I can think of,' Raden agreed.

'The tiger and the Komodo dragon!' Baruti joined them, his arrow ready in its bow.

'It sounds as if many strange things have been happening on this here island. We must destroy this tree, and I have a wee plan,' Fisk said, winking at Sari.

'Netro, Sari, Raden, Chuma; take these men into the forest,' he said, pointing to the men lying unconscious at their feet. 'When they wake up, force them to show ye where the tree is. Ye will need to burn it down. The fire will attract the men from the village and while they're distracted, Baruti and I will go to the beach and free the men that are sent on patrol to drug the white whale before they drug him again. My men inside the prison will rise up and set everyone free and join us on the beach.'

Netro listened carefully. 'And then what?'

'Come back to the beach as soon as ye have killed the plant. We'll need ye te help us free the whales.'

'What are you going to do?' asked Netro.

'We will break in te the hut next door where they keep the weapons and feed them te the prisoners through the hole in the wall.'

Sari saw a flaw in Fisk's perfect plan. 'What about the patrol of men who are to drug the mother and the baby whale?' she asked.

He smiled at her. 'I'm glad ye are with us, Sari child, ye are a clever girl.'

She smiled shyly at his praise.

'That patrol leaves from the same prison. They've agreed to pretend to drug the mother and the baby whale, and then they'll wait for our signal before attacking their captors and joining us.'

The man at Sari's feet stirred.

'Go quickly,' Fisk urged. 'I'll see ye on the beach.'

'May the goddess watch over you,' Sari said, feeling rushed and uncertain.

Chuma took one of the man's arms at her feet, and she took his other arm and helped him drag their prisoner deeper into the cover of the forest.

She heard Fisk reply as she dragged her load away, 'And also with ye, child.'

Netro and Raden followed Sari and Chuma, dragging their man behind them.

She motioned to Chuma. 'He's waking up. Quickly, find something to tie him.'

He seemed to understand as the panic rose in her chest. Chuma grabbed some twine hanging from a tree and cut a piece, quickly tying the hairy man's hands and feet. The man groaned, and Sari put her hand over his mouth.

'Something for his mouth, quickly,' she said, gesturing.

The man stirred, sinking his blunt teeth into Sari's palm.

'Ouch,' she yelled, striking him across the face with her open palm. Her eyes widened; she had never in her life hit anyone.

Raden grabbed the man roughly by his long black hair, pulling his head back from his shoulders while putting his finger to his lips in a gesture of silence. The man bared his teeth and growled. Raden pulled out his knife and showed it to the man, waving it in front of his face. The aggression went out of the villager's eyes, and Sari saw his fear lying near the surface. She turned away, reminding herself what monsters these men were for taking her mama and papa prisoner, for the killing of the whales and for the destruction they had caused. Chuma bound the villager's mouth and helped to tie the other man. Netro then tried to question the man while Raden held the knife to his face.

'Yeva, tell us where,' bullied Netro.

At the word yeva, Sari saw the recognition in her prisoner's eyes, and she knew he understood that they wanted him to take them there. The man shook his head. Netro threatened him again, but he wouldn't help them, his eyes never leaving the knife. The other prisoner stirred and Netro tried the same tactics, but they got very little response. Neither of the villagers was willing to show them where the yeva tree grew.

Sari had an idea. 'Check their bodies and see what else they have on them.'

Netro checked under their loincloths, Sari looked away, embarrassed by their maleness. In a small pouch under his loincloth, each man carried a hollow reed.

Netro handed one to her while he studied the other one. Sari looked down the reed's hole; she could see a dart held within its case. She tried to tap it out, but Chuma snatched it from her. Pointing the reed toward one of the men he put it in his mouth, showing Sari how one blew the dart into its victim. The villager with the dart pointing at him shouted and turned away, cringing. Chuma lowered his hand and then repeated the gesture, getting the same response. The four companions looked at one another, realisation setting in.

'The tip must be poisoned with the yeva plant sap,' whispered Sari.

'Looks like it,' said Netro.

Chuma threatened the man once more with the blow dart.

'Show us where the yeva tree is,' commanded Netro.

The villager nodded his head furiously in defeat, pointing wildly with his stubby, hairy finger to a place unknown farther down the track, deep into the forest. The other villager kept silent, his eyes darting around like a caged animal's. They untied both men's legs and with their arms still tied, held them roughly by each arm and marched them deeper into the forest along the forest track. Sari trailed behind the group, listening for any sounds which were not part of the forest.

They marched at a steady pace past several large trees, many of their trunks blotched with lichen. Some had fungus sticking out from their branches, but none looked very special to Sari. She bent to scratch another red itchy bump on her calf, and then took a pinch of fertile red soil between her fingers, staining them. Tiny white flowers with blue centres were dotted throughout the undergrowth.

They hadn't walked for long when they entered an open space where a circle of trees had been felled at their trunks, leaving stumps for seats. The stumps it seemed waited for an audience to witness the beauty of the largest tree Sari had ever seen which stood centre stage. The yeva tree's shiny silver trunk stretched to the heavens, shimmering in the moonlight. Sari stepped over the tree's dark silver roots, which erupted from the ground like a volcano, and walked around the thick trunk. She climbed up onto one of the roots, and walked along it toward the tree's trunk and touched its smooth bark. A silvery powder covered her hand like moth dust. Coiled tightly around the silver trunk a vine of inky purple snaked and pulsed its way to the very top where leaves of bright purple shone under the stars. Sari didn't want to burn this beautiful tree down. She suspected it was created this way so that no one would want to harm its beauty. Dark purple sap oozed from its nodules.

'Deadly, but beautiful, how did it get here?' she said aloud as she caressed the tree's smooth bark.

'I don't know, but don't touch the sap,' Raden reminded her over his shoulder as he helped the others to gather leaves.

They wasted no time by taking in the tree's glory. They tied the villager's feet once more and set about making piles of leaves all around the base of the tree. Sari reluctantly helped collect dry leaves and wood and kept herself busy building up the piles.

'Are we sure we are doing the right thing?' she asked.

'Sari, beautiful things can be deadly. Remember the butterflies,' Raden said, wagging his finger at her.

She shuddered inwardly at the thought of the butterflies. 'Yes, but surely Mother Nature must have created this.'

Raden grinned cheekily. 'Then Mother Nature will save the tree if it is truly her creation.'

Sari nodded, outnumbered. They gave her no time to consider her or their options.

When the circle of unlit fires was complete, Chuma worked diligently on lighting the pile of leaves and twigs in front of him. He rubbed his hands together as quick as lightning, rubbing one smaller branch inside another larger one. As his branch started to smoke, he added some dry leaves and blew gently.

Netro and Raden worked on the piles in front of them. They looked over to one another now and then to check on each other's progress. It took some time, and Sari thought maybe the goddess would save the tree after all.

'We must get this fire going quickly and go back to the beach. Please Sari, help us light a pile,' Netro urged, his face strained.

Sari sat before a pile on the other side of the tree. She looked up at the majestic tree before her. The tree's purple leaves seemed to dip down to greet her in the slight breeze, and on closer inspection, she realised the leaves were shrivelled and dry like they needed a good dose of rain.

'I'm sorry,' she murmured.

A pop and a crackle sounded from Chuma's pile of leaves, he cupped his hands and blew into the leaves, the smoke slowly turned to fire, and the flames licked upwards through the first pile of twigs and leaves. Chuma stoked his fire, keeping it going until it was well lit. He scrambled over to the next pile, repeating the process.

Raden and Sari's piles finally exploded into flames, and Netro looked over to Sari and shrugged. She thought he would snap his sticks in anger and considered offering him her help, but Raden shot her a look of warning. She busied herself with stoking her fire. Finally, Netro let out a cry of relief as the flames took hold of his pile. They each took charge of another pile and got to work. Sari took a quick look over at the bound men. Fear and defeat shone in their eyes. With all the piles now alight, they stood back and watched as the ring of fire danced around the trunk of the majestic tree, scorching its roots first and then leaping up its silver trunk. The vine caught alight, and the flames snaked around the tree where it twisted. Sari looked on, surprised that the fire took so well to a live tree, but the vine seemed to act like some kind of conductor and had the tree in its vice-like grip. Sari reminded herself that this was no ordinary tree. The flames darted higher, finally reaching the dry purple leaves. The leaves reminded Sari of shooting stars as they popped and crackled overhead.

* * *

They stood and watched for a long time, mesmerised by the flames as they engulfed the silvery trunk. It smelled like burnt fruit, and Sari looked sadly towards Raden.

He gave her a sympathetic smile. 'We should get going. Nothing will stop it now.'

He was right, Sari thought; the tree had succumbed entirely to its fate.

When they were sure nothing could put out the fire, they untied the men's feet and dragged them once more down the forest track, back towards the prison. As they approached the prison the noise ahead told Sari that the revolt was in full swing. A poisonous dart whizzed past Sari's ear as she helped to tie their prisoners to a nearby tree. She got out her bow and arrow ready to attack, but it seemed the prisoners had already overcome their captors. When they approached, the prison guards were being restrained by a bedraggled bunch of freed men.

All eight of Fisk's men greeted them. 'We are to follow the orders of the boy Netro,' the leader of Fisk's group said.

Their leader had blond hair and piercing blue eyes like Fisk's, but Sari could tell by his accent that he wasn't from the same place as Fisk.

Netro stepped forward and answered proudly, 'I am him. What is the update here?'

'We have overcome our captors, a sorry bunch really; didn't put up much of a fight, sir, I'm afraid. They have all been restrained as you can see. Two parties of prisoners were taken to the beach to sedate the whales before the revolt. As you know, one party will pretend to drug the mother and the baby whale,' he said formally.

'Good, are any of your men injured?'

He straightened his broad shoulders proudly. 'No.'

'What about the other prisoners that you have released?'

'They have been mistreated, and some have been in there a long time, but all are willing to help. A few of the elderly men will stay here to guard over the village and the captured villagers,' he explained.

The rescued men grouped behind Fisk's men, and Sari searched their faces for her papa.

'To the beach then!'

'Wait a minute,' Sari said.

Netro clenched his fists. 'What is it?'

'Let me quickly check something.'

She hurried over to the prison with Raden following closely.

'Are you looking for your papa, Sari?'

'You know me so well.' She smiled. 'I just need to check the few men that are staying behind. Papa may have aged.'

'Good idea; come on.'

They approached the captured villagers, and a few elderly men huddled together with broad grins on their faces turned to them. Sari looked at each one carefully.

'We are looking for someone called Avi,' Raden explained.

The men did not understand their language, merely shaking their heads instead of answering. Sari and Raden had a quick check around to make sure they had missed no one, and with a heavy heart, she re-joined Netro and the others.

Netro led the way with his head held high. Sari had never seen him so alive. She meanwhile felt terrified, quickly searching the faces of the group of freed prisoners for her papa again as they passed. These men were from all different tribes, all distinct in size, shape and colour. None of them was as tall and broad as Fisk and his men. They hurried down the sandy track toward the beach. Sari's heart thumped in her chest. They came across Fisk and Baruti who had overcome the two villagers that had escorted one of the parties on whale duty. The party of mostly bedraggled men stood limply beside Fisk and Baruti in stark contrast to Fisk's and Baruti's men who were always fierce and proud. Sari wondered how long these men had been enslaved; perhaps it had not registered to them that they were free. She worried about her papa. *Would he be like these men? If so, how long would it take a man to come back after his spirit had been crushed?*

Baruti simply nodded while Fisk greeted them warmly.

He winked at Sari. 'I was getting worried. Did everything go well?'

152

She felt more positive just seeing his rugged sailor's grin. Before she could answer him they all jumped as a section in the forest's rooftop exploded with flames.

'I see ye took care of the yeva tree, that'll keep everyone busy for a while,' Fisk chortled. 'What about the savages?'

Netro stood proudly. 'Your men have defeated the villagers and have tied them up, and this group are now free men.'

Fisk looked the men over. Sari followed his gaze and continued to scan the sea of faces for her father.

'Will ye join us men to defeat these savages and free the whales? Can ye help us te right the wrongs that are being done here?'

'We will,' they chorused.

Fisk narrowed his eyes. 'The great white whale is drug free, but he's still tied up. We must cut him loose before the savages catch on to our plan.'

Raden pointed. 'Here comes the other whale party from the next bay.'

They shouted with elation as they greeted each other.

Fisk raised his voice to the man who appeared to have taken control of the group. 'What of the female and the baby whale?'

'They are thrashing around, drug-free, but they are still restrained. What do you want me to do with these hairy beasts?'

Someone pushed forward the two villagers, their eyes wild with fear.

'Tie um up over there out of sight with the others,' Fisk spat. 'Are we all agreed on the plan to free the whales?'

'We are with you. These savages are weak; they are nothing without the yeva tree. Look at it burn.'

They turned to look at the smoke billowing from the centre of the forest's canopy.

'What was it like?' Fisk asked.

'Biggest tree we have ever seen. Purple and silver, Sari fell in love with it,' Netro teased.

Fisk winked. 'True?'

'Yes, it was very beautiful, I almost feel guilty for destroying it,' she mumbled.

'Deadly, but beautiful, like so many things on this island,' Fisk said.

'Yes, that's what Raden said.'

'Ah, he and I think alike.' He clapped Raden on the shoulder.

*T*he sight of the fire through the rooftop seemed to ignite the men's inner passion, and they responded by becoming rowdy, shouting for joy about their freedom. They made plans about which group would do what. Sari felt a little intimidated. The men introduced themselves to one another, pressing their palms together and slapping each other on the back, praising each other like comrades in arms. Adding to her unease, Sari realised that she was the only female among them. Drawn to the ocean, she walked down to the water, leaving their shouts behind her. She worried about the Holy Whale, who made not a sound. The sand felt cold as it filtered into her simple sandals. The cool breeze cut through her as it bounced off the water to greet her. The same water, blackened by night and streaked with the moon goddess's beams; the same water which held the Holy Whale captive.

"Hello, child. Finally, you are here."

10

WE ARE ALL CONNECTED

*S*ari looked behind her and saw no one. Shaking her head, she smiled to herself. *My imagination is tricking me*, she thought. The water in front of her shifted. The great white whale lifted his huge white face out of the water. She stepped back in the cold sand, startled, staring into his huge, black, almond-shaped eyes.

The Holy Whale's eyes looked tired and sad to her. "Your name is Sari, isn't it?"

'Yes,' she whispered, looking back at the men farther up the beach, feeling foolish.

The voice spoke again. "You must forgive me. My mind is foggy."

She realised the Holy Whale had spoken to her, but his mouth didn't move. She studied him carefully. Perhaps he talked to her in her mind. *Maybe she imagined it...*

"You are not imagining it, Sari, I really am communicating with you," he answered in her mind.

His voice was soothing, and she felt calm, even though she knew it should alarm her that a whale was talking to her.

He tilted his massive head to one side. "You received my pearl?"

She felt confused. 'Your pearl?'

"You need to speak with me through your mind," he urged.

You can read my mind?

He shifted his massive body in the water. "Don't worry, only those thoughts which are meant for my understanding."

Thank the goddess for that, Sari thought.

"How did you locate me without the pearl?" he questioned again.

She looked at him blankly, willing her mind to think clearly.

Why, we followed the map, of course, she said in her mind, hoping he could understand her. Then she realised. *Oh, I see! The map, yes, the pearl, I see.* She finally understood.

He dipped his head under the water. "Why yes, the giant clam made it especially for you from me, so you could find me I sent others, but they must not have been found."

She crouched down in the sand. *Thank you, I guess.* She struggled to understand. *But why me?*

"I knew you would search for your parents."

Yes, but it was Netro's idea to find you, not mine.

She didn't want the credit for something that she felt wasn't owed to her.

"The complexities of families are familiar to me, Sari. You know that they would not have left without your blessing, and I knew that you would not let them leave without you."

How did you know about my parents? She didn't feel all that surprised.

"My kingdom is full of many ears and eyes."

I still don't understand why you chose us.

"In the ocean, we have not forgotten our connection to one another. Each of us understands the role that we must fulfil. We respect one another's position, and we do not ignore the circle of life. After meeting your parents, they impressed me with their..."

'You saw my parents?' she said aloud, cutting him off.

"I carried them here, Sari. He bobbed. I saw into their hearts, into their life."

That was you, thank you, but why did you come here?

"I was on my way here after receiving some distress signals from my mate who had been captured. I have been captured here once before, but I got away. Not so this time." His eye swivelled.

I'm sorry.

"I am sorry too. I believe my mate's distress signals caused the tidal waves, and my distress signals have caused even further damage to the surrounding islands."

No, this is not your fault, she said in her mind, waving her hand around, embarrassed about the surrounding destruction.

"You are not responsible for this tribe's actions, Sari. Until I met your parents, I had wrongly concluded that all humans had forgotten about the circle of life and how we all need each other. I see now it is not so. Whales everywhere have been avoiding the island. That's why you have not seen us for a while. Whales driven by lack of food have come close to the island, only to be captured. You see, child, we are all connected; if we lose that connection we lose everything."

She swallowed over the lump in her throat. She couldn't think of anything else to say and wished Netro were here to see this. After all, it was his whale.

"I'm ready to leave now, Sari. My family waits for me."

I'll get Netro, she said, turning to go.

The Holy Whale shifted in the water. "He is coming."

Netro, Raden, Chuma, and a small group of men came running toward her.

'Sari?' Netro called.

'He's ready to go now,' she whispered.

Netro narrowed his eyes. 'The Holy Whale spoke to you?'

She shook her head as she didn't want to upset her brother.

'I feel he's ready,' she said, toeing the sand.

'He's only held by twine now. You're right, it's time to cut him free.' He sighed. 'Fisk and his men have gone to free the mother and the baby whale, and the rest of the men are keeping guard at the entrance to the beach. Let's get started.'

He waded into the water with several of the other men. A man ran along the beach toward them, yelling as he ran.

'Wait, Netro, someone is calling out, something has happened,' Sari called.

'Netro, wait, you must wait,' the man yelled in their own tongue.

Sari, recognising her papa's voice, exchanged looks with Netro who squinted through the dark of the night.

'Wait, Netro, it's Papa! You must not enter the water. Wait!'

Their papa yelled again as he raced towards them with Baruti running alongside him.

'Papa!' Sari ran to meet her papa, flinging herself into his arms.

He panted loudly for breath.

'It was you, the man on the beach,' cried Sari, looking gratefully at Baruti.

She knew he had found her papa for her. Her words didn't seem to register with her papa.

He talked over her as he hugged her, grabbing Netro by the arm. 'Netro, can you communicate with the whale?' he shouted.

'Er no, but I can try.' Netro dropped his enthusiasm for greeting his father and obeyed him.

Sari recognised the urgency in her father's voice. 'What is it, Papa?'

Again, he didn't look directly at her.

'Tell the whale not to sing out when you free him,' he shouted.

'Okay.' Netro looked bewildered but turned to the whale and told him what his papa had said. There was no response.

'No, you must try with your mind,' Papa Avi urged.

Sari watched as Netro squeezed his eyes together tightly for a minute and then opened them and looked hard at the whale.

'I'm sorry, Papa. He communicates with Fisk. I can go and get him,' he offered, dejection clear in his voice.

'There is no time. Sari, what about you, will you try?' her father begged.

She looked away from Netro's searching eyes.

'Why, Papa?' she said.

He didn't answer her.

'Why Papa?' she shouted, finally getting his attention.

He looked directly at her. 'I can no longer hear. I am deaf. The whale cries have damaged my ears and the ears of many other men here. You must tell him not to cry out in distress when you free him, or you will lose your hearing too,' he shouted on the wind.

Sari felt her stomach turn over. She was about to free the whale which had deafened her father. Her father must have understood her reluctance.

He took her face in his cupped hands. 'It is not the whale's fault, Sari; he has been in distress. We must do what we can to help him, to help us all.'

She nodded, tears springing to her eyes. Raden stood with her, giving her arm a quick squeeze. She turned back to the Holy Whale and stared once more into his eyes, commu-

159

nicating the message with her mind. He spoke again to her sadly.

'He understands and is sorry,' she reported. 'He says he will be quiet; he will communicate with the mother whale to be silent when the other men come to free her.'

'I hope it's not too late,' Papa Avi said aloud.

They waited.

'He says it is safe to go in now,' she said.

Chuma grinned broadly at her.

Netro looked at her in wonder. 'He spoke to you?'

Sari shrugged.

'Netro free him quickly; do it now,' Papa Avi said to his son.

Netro dived into the water fully clothed, and Sari waded into the icy waves after him with her knife in her hand. She looked back at her papa on the sand, and he gave her an encouraging nod. *Is he afraid to enter the water?* She wondered.

When the water reached her waist, she dived in under the icy waves and resurfaced gasping for air. She ducked under once more, searching through the blackness. Sari couldn't see the twine and felt her way along the whale's body. She touched his white, cold, rubbery skin. It glowed like the moon under the water. She felt some twine wound tightly around the base of one flipper and gingerly ran her fingers along the lines of where it began and ended. She cut the twine with her knife, the blade sawing back and forth, gradually cutting through its sinews. The cord cut deeply into the whale's skin, and she felt the flaps of the wounds as she cut through the twine. She came up for air, gasping.

Raden swam up beside her. 'What's the matter?'

'The twine is wound so tightly that when I release it, it opens up fresh wounds. He's bleeding. I'm worried about sharks,' she gasped.

'The prisoners know where the twine is; get them to

show you where to cut and pass the word around to be quick, and Sari...'

'Yes,' she said, looking into his worried face.

'Please be careful.'

'I will,' she gasped.

One man directed her in the black water to the whale's tail. Sari clung to the whale's hard, broad tail as she cut more twine with the man alongside her. The rear had been heavily bound, and she was careful not to nick the bumps and scales which covered his tail. She could not see the whale's blood in the darkness, but she smelt it and felt the warmth of it as it spurted from the wounds. Sari tired quickly, and when she thought she had done as much as she could, she swam back to shore and waited with her papa. He sat with his arm around her shoulders, his dry body warming hers. They sat together and watched in silence as Netro, Baruti, and the others swam around the Holy Whale, making sure all they had cut all the twine free.

Sari kept a close eye on Raden and Chuma, concerned now for their safety, and relief swept through her when they finally came out of the water.

Someone yelled, 'Shark!'

Netro swam below the surface.

'Oh, goddess no,' Sari gasped.

Several powerful arms sliced through the water back to the shore. Baruti was with them.

'Where's Netro?' she yelled.

Baruti looked among the faces on the beach. 'I last saw him near the tail.'

Raden dived back into the water to warn his friend.

'Raden, no,' she shouted.

Raden swam past the belly of the Holy Whale towards the

tail. Netro surfaced on the other side as the shark circled the whale's tail.

'Netro, keep still. Don't move! There's a shark near the tail,' called Raden.

Both men bobbed quietly on either side, waiting for the shark to make a move. Sari heard the Holy Whale's calm voice in her head. 'Have no fear, Sari, I will let no harm come to your brother.'

The white whale's tail emerged from the water, rivulets of water running down its sides as it rose. Sari saw the bloodied wounds sharply contrasting with the chalky white of its tail. With a powerful flick, the whale's tail crashed on top of the unsuspecting shark.

Netro and Raden swam quickly to shore, joining the others on the beach.

Netro flopped down in the sand as if nothing had happened. 'He is free of twine and it's up to him now.'

Raden grinned.

Sari shook her head.

'Thank you, my friend!' Netro laughed.

'Don't thank me. Thank him.' Raden pointed to the Holy Whale who thrashed from side to side, his tail whipping up and down behind him.

He seemed to make no progress. Sari shivered in the ocean breeze, her tunic clinging to her like ice. The Holy Whale spoke to Sari, making her jump.

"I will need your help once more, Sari."

She stood up.

'What is it?' her father and brother asked in unison.

'He's having trouble turning. He needs our help, as he's very weak now without the yeva sap.'

Several eyes turned to her. Baruti asked no questions and sent Chuma immediately to get some help.

'How do you know?' Netro asked.

Sari rolled her eyes.

'Oh right, sorry, I forgot you are the chosen one,' he drawled sarcastically.

Within minutes, Chuma returned with the rest of the freed prisoners. There were now about forty men who waded into the water with Netro leading. Sari joined them with Raden and peered into the murky water, her teeth bumping and grinding as much from the cold as from the thought of more sharks. She took her place at the whale's head, and to her surprise, her father waded into the water and joined her.

'I don't have to go under,' he said.

Sari looked nervously back up the beach. 'No one is watching the entrance.'

'We can't worry about that now,' soothed Raden.

'Ready, push!' Netro yelled above the roar of the waves.

They heaved and pushed with their combined strength. The Holy Whale shifted slightly.

'You two, you and you.' Netro pointed to about half of the group. 'Swim down with me and dig. The rest of you count to sixty and push again.'

They counted as Netro had instructed.

'Push,' yelled Raden after they had counted.

Again, they pushed, and the whale began to move. Netro and his men resurfaced and helped to push him a little farther out until he turned slightly.

On Netro's instructions, they swam under again and kept digging, while the other group counted.

'Again, push.'

They helped to turn him around, ripples of water cascading down his white back.

'Push.'

'Regroup to the rear,' Netro yelled.

The men swam to join Sari and the others at the whale's tail.

'Now push,' Netro yelled.

With a great heave they pushed, and his large body surged forward, and he moved away from the beach.

'Luckily, he wasn't in too deep, 'Netro puffed, water dripping into his eyes.

'You were amazing, Netro.'

'Thanks, Sari.'

He dunked her playfully under the water, and she splashed him as she came up. They turned back to the open sea and watched the Holy Whale swim gracefully to the bay's exit. Behind them came shouts of anger, and they turned to see a group of tribal men running toward them wielding clubs and lit torches.

'Get ready, men, here they come,' yelled Netro as they swam for the shore and their weapons.

Sari crouched down ready with her bow, lining up her first arrow, Chuma and Baruti crouched beside her, bows at the ready. Netro and Raden took out their knives, and Netro handed a spare knife to his papa.

'Wait behind us,' Baruti instructed.

The group of prisoners looked to Netro.

'Do as he says. We will hold them off for as long as we can,' Netro said.

*S*ari sensed the men were not happy about having to wait; they wanted revenge on the men that had captured them. She could feel the energy of them behind her like caged monkeys. The men came, wielding clubs, grunting and shouting with spittle flying from their fleshy lips. Just behind the front row, upon a crudely made throne of wood and twine, sat the ugliest man Sari had ever seen. Four men carried him; they did not put him down in the sand and swayed under the weight. Abog was a small man, upon a large throne, with a bent face.

'That must be Abog,' Sari said.

Abog held up his stubby left hand, and his men fell silent. A one-eyed man stepped forward to his left and called out in his crude voice.

'He's speaking my language with his foul tongue,' Baruti said. He listened, frowning.

'He wants to know what tribe we are from and what our plans are. Should I tell him?'

'Yes, I want him to know who caused his downfall,' Netro replied.

Baruti spoke for a few moments. Spittle flew from Abog's mouth in anger.

The one-eyed man spoke again.

'What's he saying?' Netro snapped.

Baruti looked at the floor. 'You should not believe his lies.'

'What is it?'

'He lies that he deals with two men from your tribe, that they trade with him in whale oil and he claims they would be very upset to hear what we are doing here. He shook his head. This cannot be true.'

Sari, Netro, and Raden exchanged looks.

'Whale oil? I don't think anyone in our tribe knows anything about whale oil.'

'He also said that Abog is a fierce man, that he took out his eye the last time outsiders didn't do as Abog asked, and he said he would like to keep his other eye.'

'Ask him about the whale oil,' Netro snapped.

They watched Baruti's face as he exchanged words with the man. His nose twitched, and his lip curled up in one corner. Sari knew he didn't like what he heard.

'They burn the whale's blubber to make oil, to light lanterns and make soap.' Baruti shrugged.

Sari paled. 'Soap, lanterns?'

'We don't understand. Ask him the names of these men,' Netro said impatiently.

They all understood the one-eyed man's response.'Ira, Fetu.'

'Are these your men?' Baruti asked, raising his eyebrow.

Sari responded for him. 'Yes, they are two of our tribal elders.'

Sari shook her head as she bit her lip.

Abog threw back his head and laughed, spittle flying from his mouth as he spoke

Baruti's face tightened. 'He claims that many seasons ago these elders helped to pay for the magical yeva tree sapling which came from across the sea. This deal they made to keep your people out of the forest.'

Netro's body shook. 'Tell him these men are evil and do not belong in our tribe. We are here to free the whales and to stop this trade, and we have burned his precious yeva tree to the ground and will fight them if we must.'

Abog let out a guttural howl, and his men responded with shrieks and scowls, charging forwards across the sand. Before Sari had time to think, Baruti let his first arrow fly and the small group of men behind followed his lead. Sari quickly positioned her arrow and aimed it at one of the men's legs. It struck his thigh, and he stumbled, falling forward. Rolling in the sand, clutching his leg in agony, he shook his fist towards her.

'Good and again, Sari, remember the bats,' encouraged Baruti.

She quickly pulled another bow from her quiver and lined it up along her string. The arrow flew through the air along with the others' arrows.

The first row of victims fell to their knees. The tribal men were nearly upon them. Abog and his throne had fallen back towards the back of the crowd.

'Quickly, one more round of arrows and then fall back,' Netro shouted. 'Get ready, men.'

Sari wondered if Netro knew how unnecessary his words were as he charged forward with his band of men following him, armed with various weapons.

They entered the fray in the emerging light. Sari pulled out the knife Netro had made for her.

Raden ran alongside her, clutching her wrist. 'Wait here. You have done enough; this is no place for you now.'

'I must, Raden.'

'Please, just wait here a while and watch. If any of us look to be in trouble, then step in. Your eyes back here will be more helpful. You can use your arrows from here.'

He melted into the madness. Sari clasped her bow with an arrow ready to fire as she strained to see the others. She saw the flashing of knives. Men went down and got up again and clubs swung overhead. Sari heard the crack of a skull. Men groaned, men shouted and charged forward. She watched Baruti; he attacked swiftly and with precision, and he seemed to stick close to her father, which comforted her. Raden towered over Abog's people and it seemed to her that they turned from him, not sure what to do with him, their clubs ineffectual against his large frame. One brave man swung his club around Raden's mid-section bringing Raden to his knees, Sari stepped forward, unsure what to do. He wobbled to his feet and grabbed the man by his long hair, swinging him around, launching him into the crowd and knocking over two other men. Her hand flew to her mouth as she watched Chuma's cheek smashed into a stray club. Netro fell to the ground with two men on top of him.

'Raden, Netro's down,' she screamed, pointing to where he lay.

Raden turned to pull both men from Netro, who jumped to his feet ,waving his knife in front of him. Sari lined up her arrow and let it fly, piercing a man about to club Netro from behind. The man fell, clutching his back. Netro saluted her, then turned around to attack a man on his left. Raden took the man on the right. Chuma bravely fought on with his shattered cheekbone. Sari took pot-shots with her arrows as the crowd thinned. Baruti fought fiercely and swiftly, slicing through men as he charged forward. They piled up around his feet, reminding her of the bats. She noticed that a lot of the villagers were down; soon more men were lying in the sand than were standing. It looked to Sari as if they were winning. The one-eyed man sounded his horn, and the villagers started back towards Abog. Netro gave the order to chase them.

Baruti stepped in, placing his hand on Netro's shoulder. 'Let them go. They are retreating, and we need to free the other whales.'

Netro nodded. A small group of villagers fell to their knees in the sand as they were being pursued, placing their stubby hands on their heads in defeat.

'Fall back. Get some twine and tie these men together,' Netro ordered, stepping over the wounded. 'You,' he said, choosing a few men. 'Look after the wounded and join us when you can. Fisk must be having problems freeing the mother and the baby whale, so we must go quickly to the next bay.'

The remaining prisoners raced up along the beach to the next bay, led by Netro, Baruti, and Chuma. Sari gaped at these men who so readily followed her brother, who they did not know, and who had not yet reached sixteen summers in age.

Behind the pack, she ran alongside Raden, who must have been thinking a similar thought.

'He really has become a leader hasn't he,' he said.

'Yes, I'm proud of him. And I am proud of you, Sari.'

They slowed, and he took her hand in his. She blushed in the promise of light.

'We did it, Sari, we have found our families, and Netro is freeing the whales.'

'I just want to go home,' she sighed. 'I want my mama and Perak to know that Papa is alive and that we are all well.'

Raden caught her in his arms and pulled her close to his chest. Sari could feel the beat of his heart as she lifted her chin and his lips met hers. He kissed her gently, then released her and stroked her cheek.

'Not long now. It's nearly over,' he said. 'Come, let's catch up to the others.'

He pulled on her hand, and they broke into a run. Side by side they grinned at one another as they ran, following Netro and the others. Rounding the next bay, they saw Fisk waist-deep in the water.

'I was about to send someone,' Fisk yelled. 'We've untied them, and the baby is free, but the mother is stuck. She's so heavy.' He heaved. 'Come on girl,' he encouraged. 'Ye be missing some men. What happened?' He nodded to the group.

'We had some trouble on the beach where we met the lovely Abog, but it's okay now,' Netro called to him. 'We need to dig the whale out, so she can turn.'

Netro waded into the water, diving over a wave and down under the water to the mother whale. Baruti and a few others followed him ,with the remaining men wading into the water to join Fisk and his men. When Netro and his men resurfaced, they started pushing. Sari stayed on the beach with her father and watched. The baby whale splashed around near his mother's body. The baby seemed distressed, and Sari worried that she would hurt someone. She tried to speak to the baby in her mind, but it was no use. Sari couldn't communicate with it. She called to the Holy Whale in her mind.

We are having trouble freeing the mother whale. You must calm the baby, or he will hurt someone, she thought.

"I will come to him," his soothing voice replied in her head.

No, please, the bay is too small for you. Stay where you are, and just talk to him, she pleaded.

The baby continued to thrash about. Suddenly, the baby whale stopped splashing in distress and turned toward the bay's exit. The baby stayed perfectly still and waited.

'She be free,' Fisk yelled.

Sari turned back to watch the mother whale turn around and collect her baby to her side. Mother and baby swam side by side to the safety of the Holy Whale that waited at the entrance of the bay.

* * *

*D*awn broke as the whales left the bay, and the group watched in awe as the whales dived under the water. After a few minutes they breached in unison, with a great splash of their tails as if in salute, Sari thought.

Sari ran to Netro and Raden as they exited the water and hugged them both.

'The alarm has been raised and we need to get away,' called Baruti.

'Go, child,' Fisk said warmly.

'Thank you, Fisk.'

'Thank ye lass, ye grandpapa would be proud.'

'There is something I need to do first,' she said smiling.

She crouched down, unslinging the bow from her shoulder. She placed it in the water and bash edit, rubbing it with sand.

Baruti let out a hearty laugh. 'I see you remember my words about a woman's curse.'

'I hope this works; we don't want Montsho shooting crooked,' she said, and giggled.

'You are a fine shot. I will tell Montsho of your bravery,' he said more seriously.

She handed the bow and quiver with the arrows back to him, dripping.

*H*er father took her arm as horns sounded in the distance. She looked at her papa beside her as he stared out to sea. She wondered if he had heard the horns, but she didn't think so. He grimaced. *He is changed somehow, and not just because of his deafness.* She studied Netro and Raden's faces, each showing something different. *Were they too changed forever,* she wondered? Sari looked back out to sea. Pods of whales could be seen in the breaking of light; joining the Holy Whale as they followed him away from the shore into safer waters. She listened to their whale cries.

11

LIFE'S KISS

*T*he savages pursued them deep into the forest, not until they had passed the dead and decaying giant Komodo dragon did the pursuit end. Weary and relieved, Sari looked up lazily to the sun overhead, shielding her eyes; she dragged her feet from exhaustion.

'We will soon reach our village,' Baruti said, looking at her sideways.

'I wonder if Fisk has reached his home yet,' she said aloud.

Baruti didn't answer her, but his words about home gave her renewed energy, and she increased her pace and gave him a grateful smile. She squeezed her papa's hand.

'Papa, we will soon all be together again. Praise the goddess for our good fortune,' she said almost to herself, knowing her father could not hear her.

He smiled briefly in her direction but glanced back towards the ever-widening track ahead. A small party of scouts from Sakima's tribe greeted them and ran off ahead to announce their arrival.

The group stumbled toward the outskirts of the village, Sari walking between her father and Raden who guided her

172

gently forward, clasping her hand in his. The track ahead filled up with well-wishers, the dark figures calling out their names, and pulling at their tunics, touching them as if to make sure they were real. A woman with wild ebony hair flung herself into Chuma's arms, and he kissed her tears away as they streamed down her face. Sari realised she knew very little about her companions. She smiled and bowed her head as once again they adorned her in necklaces made from wood, teeth, and bones. The lengthy procession line led to their leader Chief Sakima, who sat patiently upon a throne made of beautifully carved wood. Baruti and Chuma knelt before him and spoke in hushed tones as Chief Sakima questioned them intently.

Sari looked around impatiently for her mama and Perak, sensing that perhaps they had returned home to wait for them after all. She felt disappointment settle into her bones, and, looking at her father, she mouthed, 'I'm sorry.'

'If they have returned, your mama felt it best,' he shouted, causing Chief Sakima and the entire tribe to look at her papa with curiosity.

'Sorry,' he said, still loudly.

Baruti addressed him in a loud voice. 'Avi, father to Netro, Sari and Perak and life partner to Lena their mother Chief Sakima wishes to meet with you. Come forward, please.'

Sari noticed that Baruti had returned to using his formal voice. Sari's papa rose and greeted their chief. Chief Sakima rose from his throne, pressed his palm to her papa's palm in greeting and walked into his hut, gesturing for Avi to follow him. Sari did not hide her dismay, and Baruti explained to her quickly before he followed them into the hut.

'From one chief to another, they will discuss the events so far. You will stay here until called upon, then we will have a grand celebration. Your bravery will be exalted. Now I must go and interpret for them.'

'Wait, Mama and Perak; are they still here?'

'I will let you know when I know more.' He bowed slightly and slipped into the great hut.

The women of the tribe pulled on Sari, Netro, and Raden's tunics and gestured for them to follow them to the centre of the camp. They sat on grass mats and drank water from wooden bowls and ate fruits and nuts. Two women played with Sari's hair, combing it and twisting it in their style. After they had relaxed for a while, the women tried to convey that they had a surprise for Raden. They giggled in high-pitched tones and demonstrated covering their eyes before bringing forward a blindfold and wrapping it gently around his head and over his eyes. One woman got up to fetch the surprise. Sari fidgeted in her excitement.

'What is this all about?' he said.

'Maybe they have the perfect bride for you?' Netro teased back to his old self.

Raden's face paled behind the blindfold, and Netro roared with laughter.

Sari screamed when she saw what they had for him, and Raden fell backward onto the grass mat as something small and hairy launched itself into his lap. Raden tore the blindfold from his eyes and looked down.

His mouth fell open. 'Shadow fox, I thought you were dead. I don't understand...' he cried.

He regained his composure, ruffling his shadow's fur. His fox rolled over and whimpered with excitement.

Raden looked over to Sari, shaking his head. 'I can't believe it, I don't understand,' he repeated.

The women giggled behind their hands. The fox jumped up and licked at Raden's face with quick, short licks.

Baruti joined them.'I see they have reunited you with

your friend. I am told that he staggered into the village not long after we left. My people helped to heal him. When Perak returned to our village, he explained to my people about these things, shadow foxes, and how he must wait for Raden here. Perak was a great help in many situations; it was a good plan that he returned.'

Raden turned to the woman. 'Thank you.'

'Wait, what do you mean, Baruti?' Sari asked.

'It seems you were followed into the forest. Two young men were captured just after we left for our adventure. Chief Sakima is very wise; he believed they wanted to do you harm, so he kept them here. When Perak returned, he told Chief Sakima that they were troubled boys from your tribe.'

'Who?' they chorused.

'Their names are Kupe and Tama.'

'I know those boys,' said Raden.

'I can't believe it, they were sent to catch us, harm us? I know them too, they are just boys.' Sari shook her head.

Baruti ignored her. 'Raden, Chief Sakima wishes to speak with you and Netro. Sari, he does not wish to see you.'

His words stung Sari, but her head was spinning with the news of Kupe and Tama.

'I must know about my family,' she insisted.

'Your mother returned with Perak and with the rest of Raden's family. That is all I know.'

'I don't want to see the chief anyway, I only wanted to know about my mother and Perak.' She said, pulling a face behind his back as he turned from her.

'And the prisoners, Kupe and Tama?' Netro asked.

'Chief Sakima awaits your decision.'

'I'll be back soon,' said Raden, squeezing her hand.

Raden's shadow fox got up to follow Raden as he walked away with Baruti and Netro.

'He cannot enter the hut,' Baruti said, clapping his hands loudly to frighten the fox away.

Sari pulled on the fox's back to sit him next to her, and she stroked his fur. 'I'll look after him.'

She traced the scars in his fur, which had healed into angry red welts. She looked into his little round eyes and smiled. She felt content that her family was home, together, and safe. Finally, things are returning to normal, but what about Kupe and Tama?

She was not annoyed about not being invited into Sakima's hut. *The girl that had arrived here not so long ago would have minded*, she realised.

Raden's shadow wouldn't stay with her for long and approached the hut, pacing up and down outside its entrance. Sari got up, deciding to go for a walk around the village. She encouraged the fox to follow her, but he could not be tempted away from the door of the hut where his master had gone. She left him and walked off, closely followed by a group of women. She walked in front of a group of open-faced huts lined with bed mats. A man lay groaning on one mat, and as Sari approached, she saw blood oozing from a large gash in his leg. Sari's hand flew to her mouth, and she turned to the woman next to her. The woman widened her eyes and bared her teeth. Using her fingers, she bent them at the knuckles and made them into claws and growled menacingly.

'Tiger?' Sari questioned.

The woman nodded.

Something else that has returned to normal. Sari thought. *Had Jahi survived the Komodo dragon's bite?* It seemed so long ago.

'Jahi?' Sari questioned the same woman.

The woman nodded her head of black plaits toward the next hut. Sari moved to the next opening. Jahi sat propped up on his mat. He beamed to her as she entered. She smiled back with relief and went over to him and took his hand. She pressed it to her forehead to show him he had been in her thoughts. When she released his hand, he took her hand and made the same gesture. She smiled again and left him to rest and recover. Sari felt tired. Yawning loudly, she put her hand to her mouth and smiled weakly at the women accompanying her. They seemed to understand and guided her through the village to a single grass hut. Her papa would now take her place in the hut she had once shared with the boys on their first visit. Her papa would not allow her to stay in the same hut as Raden, this she knew. Sari collapsed gratefully on to the grass mat as the woman closed the door behind her. It was cool and dark inside, and she soon felt herself drifting off to sleep.

* * *

Sometime later, someone returned and shook Sari's shoulder gently. She opened her eyes to a young woman holding a lantern to her face. Sari rubbed her eyes and squinted at the light and sat up, yawning.

The woman pointed to Sari's chest. 'Sari,' she said in a soft singsong voice and then pointed to her own chest.'Deka.'

'Deka, what a lovely name,' Sari nodded.

Sari held out her palm in greeting. The woman smiled shyly. She had brought scented water for Sari, and she helped her to wash and dry. Deka combed Sari's hair with a wide-toothed comb made of bone and braided Sari's hair in a similar style to her own. She pulled and tugged at Sari's hair, forcing Sari's head to jerk from side to side. She then unfolded a grass skirt and helped Sari to step into it and placed a tie made of dried grass around her breasts.

'Oh, thank you, it is lovely.'

Sari twirled around, and Deka laughed heartily. She then

helped Sari put on all the special jewellery that they had given her as gifts. She noticed that Deka must have washed the pieces that Sari had dug up on the way back into the village. They all shone with newness. Deka then placed a beautiful yellow orchid, like the one she wore, behind Sari's left ear. She grinned and nodded in approval. One last twirl, and it was time to join the others for the celebration.

The moon goddess shone brightly above as they walked, and Sari gave her a wink. Deka led her into the centre of the village where a massive fire roared, and many villagers mingled and sat at a safe distance from the blaze. Loud cheering erupted from the crowd as Deka walked Sari past them and the roaring fire into the centre to join the others. Chief Sakima sat at the head of the gathering, elevated on his throne. He wore a feathered crown, and a robe made from animal skins. Netro, Raden and Avi sat to his right, and Baruti, Montsho and Chuma sat to his left on grass mats. She smiled at Montsho, glad to see him safe and remembering that he had helped her brother Perak. There were two spare places between Raden and Chuma. Sari firstly kneeled beside Chief Sakima, bowing her head to show respect, and then sat closest to Raden, who stared at her with his mouth slightly ajar. She smiled over to Chuma, who greeted her with a broad grin and hand on heart. She knew it must delight him to be home among his people. Her papa leaned over Raden and squeezed her hand.

'You look beautiful,' he bellowed.

'Thank you Papa, and you all look very handsome too,' she said, nodding.

Their washed hair had been tied back neatly, and their robes were made of a fine weave. Another cheer erupted as two tribesmen carried Jahi through the crowd. He did his best to bow before his chief and then took his place in between Chuma and Sari. Someone behind Sari filled her carafe with a spicy drink and melted away before she could say thank you. Chief Sakima sat forward in his chair and raised his carafe and spoke in his tongue, which sounded smooth and melodic to Sari.

Baruti interpreted after every few words spoken. 'Welcome! Let us drink to your safe return.'

They all took a sip of their spicy beverage.

Chief Sakima guzzled from his cup as Baruti continued.

'You have been courageous, and you have brought balance to our village. To my men, I will reward you with whatever your hearts' desire. To their companions, I offer you and your village our allegiance and our never-ending friendship.'

Sari followed the others' lead and got on her knees and bowed deeply.

Netro looked to his father, who lifted his head slightly and replied in a loud voice.

'We also offer our continued support and friendship. Let balance be restored forever to the forest.'

Sakima smiled as Baruti interpreted Papa Avi's words.

'Let the feast begin.'

Sakima clapped his large black hands as six village men lifted his throne from the ground.

Sari got up and followed with the others as they carried Chief Sakima past the roaring fire through the cheering crowd to his grand hut. The double grass doors were held aside for the large throne, and they placed Chief Sakima and his throne at the head of a long table which lay toward the right side of the hut. Sari's eyes lit up at the feast before her. A large wild pig created the centrepiece, surrounded by colourful fruit and nuts. She recognised the meat of bats and small rodents by their smell, and there was a display of several different fish in varying sizes. Root vegetables, some cooked and some raw, presented beautifully in assorted bright colours, along with cooked maize and grains. There were a lot of foods that Sari had never seen or eaten before, and her stomach rumbled in anticipation. They were led to the left side of the hut and encouraged to stand in line. Sakima sat on his throne and watched them.

The crowd stood silently; he nodded to Baruti, who interpreted as he spoke. 'I present this feast to you in honour of our friendship, but first, let me reintroduce you to some travelling companions.'

Sari's heart lurched in confusion, looking toward the door. Three tribesmen entered and paraded before them. Sari sighed. It wasn't her mother and Perak as she had hoped.

'These are the men you saved from the pit. They wish to thank you in the presence of their chief,' Baruti said formally, waving them along.

Each man greeted them by taking their hands in theirs and placing them over their hearts.

'You are forever connected to their hearts, and they thank you,' Baruti said.

The men said, 'thank you,' in Sari's language as they moved down the line.

Papa Avi stepped forward out of the line and turned to Chief Sakima. 'It is we who thank them for returning our family to the safety of your tribe, and we thank you, Chief Sakima, for taking our family in and caring for them.'

Baruti interpreted as Chief Sakima clapped his hands, his face beaming at Papa Avi's words.

'Let the feast begin.'

Deka approached them and guided Sari to the table. She gestured for the others to join her, and she showed them where to sit.

Sari let those around her help themselves before deciding on what she wanted. She noticed that Sakima and his men ate with the fingers of their right hand, and she reminded herself to copy this manner once she had made up her mind.

She stared at the wild boar, its beady eyes staring back at her, and she helped herself to some fish. Sari had never eaten wild boar before and struggled to look away.

'We don't get wild boar where we live. This may be your only chance to try it, it's good,' Netro grinned with a full mouth.

Sari yearned for the familiar foods from home but did not voice this. 'I guess you are right,' she said.

She had developed a new respect for her brother. He had been right about taking this journey. She looked across the table towards Raden and her father, who nodded in agreement. Netro passed her a piece of boar meat. She popped it into her mouth and chewed. It had a strong flavour, but she instantly liked it, although it took a lot more chewing than she was used to.

'So, what happened with the chief today?' she probed both boys, just a little curious.

'Ah, we had to describe everything we had seen and heard on the entire journey,' Netro said, rolling his eyes.

'It was exhausting.' Raden added through a mouthful of food.

'Why did he need to know so much?' she whispered behind her hand.

'Baruti says he longs to travel but cannot leave his tribe, so he travels in his mind through other people's stories,' Netro said, wiping his mouth with the back of his hand.

'Why didn't he want to speak with me?' Sari asked.

'I asked Baruti, and he thinks Sakima is ashamed that a woman has travelled when he can't. He would like to pretend you didn't see very much.'

Netro shovelled more food into his mouth as he spoke. Sari bristled but tried to understand the man she knew so little about. She looked over to him, and he caught her eye for a second and quickly looked away.

'You are lucky to be allowed in this hut,' Raden whispered. 'That, at least, is a concession on his part.'

'I know,' she murmured, desperate to change the subject. "Where is your shadow?'

'Two children offered to look after him. He's lucky the chief didn't cook him up for tonight's feast.'

They all sniggered.

'Do you think we can go home tomorrow?'

'I'll ask Baruti. We do not want to offend the chief,' Netro said, starting to get up.

'While you're there, ask him if I can get a second helping.' Raden laughed.

Netro shook his head. 'Always thinking of your stomach Raden.'

The boys had become men. *If they are men, I must have become a woman*, Sari thought, smiling to herself.

Her Papa took her hand. 'What are you thinking?'

She blushed. 'About the poor boar,' she lied, pointing to the pig to make sure her papa understood.

'I'll stick to my fish,' he said loudly.

Sari hoped no one had overheard who might understand and be offended. She watched Netro approach the chief who smiled with his wide mouth. Something about him reminded her of the Holy Whale. She wondered if the whale had returned home by now, and how long it would take. *Where was his home?* She smiled at the thought of his reunion with his mate and baby. She felt the goodness of their deed fill her. *Why her? Why had he been able to communicate with her?* For the first time in her life, she felt special, and she knew it wasn't because of the grass skirt she wore.

Netro re-joined them as she was finishing her bowl of food. 'We are free to go as soon as the ceremony is over, Papa.'

Papa Avi nodded. 'We should get a good night's rest and leave in the morning. We'll take Kupe and Tami with us.'

Netro nodded and sat down. Sari buzzed with excitement until a dark thought clouded her mind, and she voiced it.

'What about the giant butterflies? Oh, Mama and Perak... I had forgotten.' She put her hand to her mouth.

Papa Avi grabbed her other hand. 'I'm sure Perak hadn't forgotten, and besides, nature has been restored. You heard about a tiger attacking one of the villagers.'

'That doesn't mean everything is back as it was,' Sari said fearfully.

They fell silent as even Raden had no words of wisdom. Before they could spiral further into their fears, Sakima rose from his throne and leaned over and helped himself to another bowl of food.

'That's your sign.' Netro nudged Raden, who proceeded to fill his bowl.

Sari sat back, stretching, and looked around the hut. It was dimly lit with lanterns. The village celebrated outside, and she hoped they would join them soon.

Raden spoke quietly to her between mouthfuls. 'What is the first thing you will do when you get?'

'I will spend some time with my family and Heni.' She smiled.

'That sounds good.'

'I guess we will have to face the council,' she said, breaking off more meat and placing it in her bowl.

'What did you say?' her father questioned loudly.

She raised her voice. 'The council.'

'Your mama is a smart woman. That is why she would have returned early to smooth the waters for our return,' he assured her.

'You don't understand, there will be no council left when

Kupe and Tama tell Elder Malo what has been going on and Ira and Fetu's part in it. Our people will be happy to see us, we have done much to bring peace to our village.' Netro scowled.

Sari continued to speak loudly so her papa could understand them. 'We've still broken the rules and might be punished, and some villagers might not believe us if they don't tell the truth about Abog and the whales.'

'I'm sure your papa is correct; your mama will have seen to it, let's wait until we speak to the prisoners.' Raden seemed confident.

'What is the worst that could happen?' Netro wanted to know. 'If they try to punish us, we will leave and take some villagers with us. There will be followers, people who are grateful,' he snapped.

'Netro, no one is saying that what you did was a bad thing. I am very proud of you all. You have saved our village.' Papa Avi pushed his bowl away. 'But you know the elders are set in their ways, and we must follow their laws.'

'We'll see, things are changing papa, they have things to answer for too now,' Netro huffed.

Sari knew her brother well enough to know that there was a plan developing in his head, but for once, she trusted him, and she knew she would follow his lead.

She squeezed his hand gently. 'I am with you, whatever you decide. You are our leader.'

He seemed surprised. 'Thank you, Sari.'

'I'm with you, too,' Raden muttered as he finished his second bowl of food.

'I think you will go wherever Sari goes,' Netro drawled.

Sari blushed into her empty bowl.

* * *

*C*hief Sakima clapped once more. At the sound of his clap, the hut doors swung back and several villagers entered to clear the feast away. A loud cheer erupted from outside the hut as they exited with the leftover food. Sari assumed that the leftovers were being feasted upon outside. They lifted the chief's throne with Sakima upon it and carried him to the other side of the hut, and he waved at them to join him.

'Chief Sakima wishes for you to be seated by his throne,' Baruti announced.

Sari rose with the others and sat beside Sakima's throne at his feet. Six women entered wearing grass skirts like Sari's and with pink orchids in their hair. They stood in the centre of the hut waiting for the men with instruments to set up behind them. They smiled shyly at their audience. The music began, and the woman swayed their hips and danced slowly in a circle to the tapping beat of the drum and the melodic sounds of the flute. Sari enjoyed the women's dance until one woman pulled her up on to the floor alongside them. She blushed furiously and stood frozen, not daring to move. Another woman took her hand and showed her some steps. Sari tried to copy her and wriggled her hips uncomfortably.

Netro and Raden clapped and cheered loudly, and she poked her tongue out to them. She looked at her papa, who beamed and nodded in encouragement. She soon got into the swaying rhythm with the other woman's help and relaxed. Much to Sari's delight, Chief Sakima got up and danced alongside her. His thick waist banging from side to side. He held his arms high above his head and sashayed and swayed his way out of the hut doors into the waiting crowd. Sari followed, dancing and laughing and could hear the roar as they swept her along out into the balmy night. Everyone had now joined in. The men with the music followed and set up once more beside the roaring fire. Sari looked over towards Raden, who had invented a dance all of his own. Even Netro seemed to be relaxing and enjoying himself as he drained his carafe and saluted Sari. They danced and celebrated into the dark of night. The roaring fire had now died down to embers. There were bodies slumped everywhere from exhaustion. Sari stepped over a slumbering form and got back to her hut, where she collapsed on to her woven mat. She fell fast asleep before she could take off her grass skirt.

* * *

*a*t first light, they met Baruti and Chuma at the edge of the village. Baruti shoved Kupe and Tama towards them and spat on the ground at their feet. Their waists had been tied together, and their hands were bound. Sari's eyes slid over them. They were unharmed, but the look she gave them could have frozen their hearts. Raden's shadow fox let out a low growl.

Baruti held up his hand to each of them. 'This is goodbye.'

Sari smiled. 'Thank you for everything Baruti.'

'It was my great pleasure to travel with such worthy companions as you.' He said formally.

A single tear slid down Chuma's face.

Swallowing a lump in her throat, Sari gave him a quick hug. 'We will see you again.'

Raden took her hand, and they moved off quickly with Netro pushing the prisoners in front of them. Sari turned to see Chuma standing with a single hand raised in farewell.

* * *

*T*he season's change was upon them, and with no rain, the damp musty smell in the forest had almost gone. Dry leaves fell from the trees and scrunched under Sari's feet as she walked. The bark on the trees had dried and cracked. Netro had questioned his prisoners daily and as Sari listened in as they neared their home village, many things became clear to her. A small group of boys had been working with Ira and Fetu for many seasons. This had been expected from a young age, they had threatened their families. They had received little in the way of reward except for food for themselves and their families. Among other dirty deeds, they moved in groups and raided other villages in the forest. There had never been a trade agreement or help from other villages, the food had been taken by force. Another reason to keep their people out of the forest, Sari realised. A clearer picture was forming in her mind of these evil men and the lengths they had gone to to keep them from finding out about the whale trade. Sari felt sorry for Kupe and Tama and the other boys and worried for their future in the village, but couldn't keep her anger from rising at their selfishness.

They approached the pickets to the forbidden forest, this time though they stood on the other side about to re-enter their homeland. She was nearly home.

'Is this it?' her father questioned loudly, looking at the pickets with disgust.

'I know. Disappointing, isn't it? We all imagined a huge fence,' Sari answered and was about to repeat herself in a louder voice when he answered.

'Such madness,' he sighed.

'Papa, you just heard me.'

'Yes, I didn't want you to get too excited, but my hearing seems to be getting a little better.' He smiled.

Sari sighed happily.

'Do you want help with that?' Raden asked for the tenth time since their journey had begun.

'I'm okay,' she assured him. She was carrying with her a large butterfly wing.

'Tell me again why you want that thing?' Netro asked.

'I don't know... maybe as a reminder of our travels.' She shrugged.

He shook his head as he stepped over the pickets, pushing the two boys in front of him, taking back the lead with their father following. Raden's shadow fox ignored her as he had on the entire journey home. She caught another one of his dirty looks. She tried to pat him, but he scampered out of her reach over the pickets to join Netro.

Netro turned to wait for Raden, who stood next to Sari, staring down at the fence that had kept them home for so long. Sari made a silent promise to herself that she would never cross this line again.

'You can't blame him; you are carrying the wing of one of the creatures that tried to kill him,' Raden said, nodding toward his shadow fox.

'The butterflies were all dead when we got there, and we burned the rest of them for him to see,' she scoffed.

'I know, but why did you really bring it?' he whispered.

'I guess to show Elder Malo what we were up against. It might make him go easier on us and show them the error of their ways.'

'Are you worried for Netro?'

She looked into Raden's kind eyes. 'Yes, you know the elders will blame the ringleader, and who is to say our tribe will believe any of our stories. I don't believe Kupe and Tama will tell the truth. You must admit it will sound unreal to our people. The elders have forbidden us to talk of the Holy Whale...' Her heart felt heavy, just thinking of seeing the elders again.

'Try to focus on being reunited with your family.'

Raden was so wise, she thought.

'What are you whispering about?' Netro asked.

Raden took Sari's arm and guided her as they stepped over the pickets. 'Sari is worried the tribe and Elder Malo won't believe us and that Kupe and Tama won't tell the truth once they see Ira and Fetu.'

'You are right, they won't, but we have questions for Ira and Fetu too. I don't know how this will turn out, but there is something I haven't told you yet.' Netro sighed.

'What?' they chorused.

'Did you ever wonder why Elder Malo never stood up to Ira and Fetu and question their fine clothing or where these food supplies were coming from?'

Sari shook her head. No, she hadn't, she'd always thought he was kind and old and nothing beyond that.

He pulled Tama by the ear. 'Tell them.'

Tama screwed his face up in pain while Netro twisted.

'Ira made me put yeva sap in Malo's water.'

Sari's eyes widened. 'You really will be in trouble for that.'

'Let's keep going,' Netro said as he pushed ahead, leaving them behind.

* * *

*H*er papa had tired and lagged behind, Sari wondered if he too worried about their return. There were no scouts to greet them or announce their arrival, and there were no guards to protect their border. They had never needed to defend themselves from danger before. The forest danger had been a lie, *but maybe now it was what lay beyond the forest that they should worry about.* Sari suddenly realised as she walked along that her village was so unprepared for the evils that lay outside the pathetic picket fence. The threat had always come from the sea; the island's evil had not yet touched them. She wondered how long before that evil would come calling. She thought of the tribe on the other side of the island and shuddered inwardly, causing the giant butterfly wing to shake in her hands.

* * *

*T*he path they had made on their way out had already overgrown, and they hacked through the new branches and vines. A snake slithered across their path, and the birds twittered and called overhead. The landscape had changed so much. Sari realised that without the help of Netro and Raden, she would have surely been lost, wandering in the forest forever. She suddenly changed her mind about a shadow butterfly for herself and decided on something fiercer, like a wild boar.

As they reached Elok Creek, where their journey had begun, memories flooded her mind. They stood for a moment looking into the creek's murky water. Elok Creek flowed smaller than when they had left it because of low rainfall. They walked around it and followed the well-trodden path that led to the beach. Sari guessed her people had been relying on the creek for fresh water. It occurred to her they might meet someone along the path, and excitement whizzed through her weary body.

Sari saw that Netro had stopped on the path ahead.

'What's happen..?' Sari trailed off as she saw the men.

The elders' Ira and Fetu stood before him with a group of boys Netro's age.

'Leave Tama and Kupe with me. I banish you Netro, you must turn around now and leave,' Ira snapped, his yellow eyes flashing, his shadow snake hissing.

'These men are telling me I cannot come home, Sari.'

Tama and Kupe shrunk behind Netro.

'You think we will allow you to come back here Netro, telling your stories?' Fetu scowled, his shadow rat baring its teeth.

Ira put his hand on Fetu's shoulder to calm him, pulling away quickly when Fetu's shadow rat tried to bite him.

'I think when I tell them you have been trading with those monsters, it will be you leaving, not me,' Netro scowled.

Ira's eyes narrowed. 'Careful now boy, no one will believe you, and you will make it harder on your sister and her friend here,' he said, nodding his head toward Raden and to Sari.

'But...' Sari started.

Ira held up his hand. 'I will be forced to banish them too.'

Raden's shadow fox let out a low growl and Raden placed his hand on his head.

'Kupe and Tama will tell what they know, and the people will know that you are lying,' said Raden. 'And my grand-papa, he will tell his story of how you tried to have him and my family killed.'

'Kupe and Tama are with us, they will not speak out against their brothers,' Fetu spat.

The group of boys behind them mumbled their agreement.

'Your grandpapa is old Raden and is mistaken.' Fetu scowled.

Ira smirked. 'And if this is true, why has your grandpapa come back here and not said a word about this to anyone? People will say he is suddenly making up the tale to save you.'

'What's wrong boys, nothing to say now?' Fetu laughed.

Papa Avi pushed his way between Netro and Raden. 'They may have nothing more to say, but I do.'

The elder's eyes flicked to one another and Ira shrank back behind Fetu, his snake disappearing down his tunic.

'Avi, it is so nice to see you alive.'

'I think we can ignore the courtesies, Ira. There are two of you, and there are many of us who will tell the same story about how you traded in whale meat. And how you lied about the forest and the whales and benefited from the slaughter of those whales. I think Netro is right, and it will be the both of you that will leave right now,' he shouted.

Sari jumped. She had forgotten how stern he could be.

'Now, now, Avi, let us explain, here,' he offered him his flask, 'you've had a long journey, have a little to drink.' Ira stuttered.

Papa Avi pulled out his knife, waving it in their direction. 'You think I am stupid enough to trust you? What? Have you mixed yeva sap into that water? Now I have witnesses that will tell that you tried to poison me.'

Ira held his flask up. 'Poison, I don't know what you speak of.'

Avi thrust his knife towards Ira. 'Show me then, take a drink.'

Ira smirked, draining his flask onto the track, its purple contents pooling in the dirt.

'Smart move, but you'd better get going, or I'll tie you and your monkey here up and take you both before Elder Malo and see what he has to say.'

The group of boys behind Ira and Fetu melted into the trees behind them and took off.

'Now listen here, old man,' said Fetu, squaring his shoulders, not realising the group behind him had fled.

Netro and Raden stood shoulder to shoulder with Avi, hands on the hilts of their knives.

Papa Avi smirked, 'Yes, my boys have grown up while they've been away clearing up your mess, so I think you need to say thank you and be on your way.'

Raden's shadow fox snapped at their feet, growling. Ira

and Fetu looked fearfully at one another as they realised they were alone.

'Surely you don't expect us to go now,' they choroused.

'Yes now.' Papa Avi thrust his knife towards them once more. 'And Tama and Kupe will stay with us.'

Fetu spat in the dirt at their feet.

'All right, we'll go, but we'll be back,' Ira growled, putting his hands in the air and backing away. 'Come Fetu.'

Fetu scowled as his rat ran around on the top of his head. Papa Avi pointed the way with his knife, and they shuffled slowly off.

'Never come back, and if you come across a tribe headed by Chief Sakima, I'd keep moving along, he doesn't like your kind,' he called after them.

* * *

*T*he group didn't speak as they continued on. Sari hung her head, but when they broke through the trees onto the beach, she felt the relief shudder through her slight frame. She stepped out onto the scorching sand; children splashed and played down near the water. They had arrived unannounced, and no one seemed to notice them at first as they made their way down to the sea. Sari caught sight of her younger brother, Perak. He turned to see them as if sensing their arrival.

'Sari, Netro, Papa!'

He ran to greet them, huffing and puffing as he threw himself into his papa's arms first and then Sari's.

He squeezed her tightly and looked up at her with awe in his eyes. 'You're home,' he gasped.

She beamed. 'I made a promise, didn't I? And you've grown.'

He beamed. 'I've been thinking about what shadow animal I want.'

'Oh, yes?'

'I want a shadow whale.'

Sari laughed and ruffled his hair. 'Well, we'll have to wait and see.'

Other villagers turned to the sound of their shouting. A mob of people surrounded them. They touched and pulled at their clothing as if they were a vision. Lena pushed through the crowd, leaping into her husband's arms and then hugging her children tightly to her.

She looked deeply into Sari's green eyes, which matched her own, and kissed Sari on the forehead. 'I knew you would bring us all back together.'

Heni called out to Sari, 'My friend.'

Sari hugged her. 'Thank you, Heni; you were so brave; did you get into trouble?'

'No, it helped that my mother is related to Elder Malo. I'm so glad to see you,' she gushed.

Raden's grandpapa pressed his nose to Raden's.

'I have much to tell you, Grandpapa.' Raden whispered.

Aunts and uncles embraced them, and everyone talked and shouted over one another.

'Tell us what happened?' they cried.

'We have much to tell all of you, but we must see Elder Malo first,' Netro cried back in response.

A runner went to fetch Elder Malo. He ambled down the beach toward them, surrounded by the boys from the forest, who spoke with him frantically, their arms gesturing, their eyes wide and their faces pinched. Malo nodded his matted grey hair in response to their pleas.

He stood before them now, sweat dripping into his pale blue eyes which crinkled at the corners.

'Welcome home to all of you.' Elder Malo threw his arms wide. 'It is good to see you alive Avi,' he smiled, as they embraced.

Malo pressed his palm to Raden's and nodded. 'I see you may have found your own wife, so we must talk later.'

Raden dropped Sari's hand, and Sari blushed as she pressed her palm to Malos, her butterfly wing forgotten by her side.

Malo's eyes widened. 'Brave girl,' he said, nodding to the wing.

'We have so much to tell you,' she said.

'I know. I'm sorry that Ira and Fetu are not yet here to greet you. I don't know where they are.' A smile pulled at the edges of his mouth as he looked around.

As Netro pressed his palm to Malos, Netro whispered, 'we have already seen Ira and Fetu on the path in.'

Malo smiled. 'So I hear from my friends,' he said, gesturing to the boys crowding around him. 'It seems they don't share my enthusiasm for your adventures, but don't worry about them now. I am also told from others that the three of you are heroes.'

'We have a lot to tell you, but I don't think you will see Ira and Fetu again,' Netro said.

'I understand. And why are these boys tied up?'

'There is good reason...' Netro stammered.

*T*ama and Kupe fell to their knees in the sand at Elder Malo's feet, and he placed a hand on each of their heads. 'Many stories have come to my ears over the last few suns dear boys, and it seems we have all been under one spell or another.'

'Forgive us,' they cried.

Malo held up his hand. 'We have much to discuss, but later,' Malo sighed.

'I don't understand; you don't want me to explain now, I can tell you our story and theirs?' Netro said.

Elder Malo swept his hand in the ocean's direction. 'This explains everything we need to know for now.'

The crowd parted, and they looked toward the sea where dozens of whales frolicked in their waters, many with calves beside them. The Holy Whale took centre stage, breaching out of the water, its brilliant white body glistening in the sunlight. The Holy Whale dove back down into the ocean's depths, its massive tail flapping and crashing through the water creating a great splash.

The villagers clapped and cheered.

Sari took Raden's hand in hers and smiled up into his kind dark eyes.

They were home.

ENJOYED THIS BOOK?

Thanks for joining Sari and her companions on their adventure. If you enjoyed this book, a review would be much appreciated as it helps other readers to discover the story.

If you want to know when my new books are being released, you can sign up for my Reader's List here:

www.selenajane.com/contact

ACKNOWLEDGMENTS

Let's start at the beginning…

To my mum for exploring all things spiritual with me from a young age and instilling in me the belief that I can do anything I put my mind to.

Thanks to my dad, who with his natural enthusiasm, taught me to appreciate the miraculous wonders of nature and for introducing me to Sir David Attenborough when I was a child.

Much love to my brother who without realising it makes me want to be a better person.

I'm so very grateful for my family, Craig, Eve and Fletcher for their love. For always believing in me and especially for their excitement about publishing my first novel, it's been a long time coming and they've never wavered in their support.

Thanks to my editor Sally for her wisdom and thoughtful comments.

I'm grateful to my cousin Emma for helping with the final proofread and helping me to believe I was ready.

A heartfelt thank you to Hannah for being so easy to work with on the design of the cover.

I also really appreciate those family members and many friends who have supported me on social media, its be a long journey and you've stuck with me.

A final shout out to my animals who've been at my feet for every word written, you've made the journey to the final chapter less lonely.

Lightning Source UK Ltd.
Milton Keynes UK
UKHW011318210223
417314UK00004BA/322